"Would you like to hold the baby?"

Carson began to answer no, that the joy of being the first to hold this new life belonged to Lori. But one look at the tiny being and he knew he was a goner. He fell hard and instantly in love.

"Yes," he murmured, and took the infant in his arms.

The baby was so light, she felt like nothing. And like everything. Carson had no idea that it could happen so fast, that love could strike like lightning and fill every part of him with its mysterious glow. But it could and it had.

Something stirred deep within him, struggling to rise to the surface. Self-preservation had him trying to keep it down, push it back to where it could exist without causing complications.

"She's beautiful," he told Lori. "But then, I guess that was a given."

Dear Reader,

Oh, baby! This June, Silhouette Romance has the perfect poolside reads for you, from babies to royalty, from sexy millionaires to rugged cowboys!

In Carol Grace's *Pregnant by the Boss!* (#1666), champagne and mistletoe lead to a night of passion between Claudia Madison and her handsome boss—but will it end in a lifetime of love? And don't miss the final installment in Marie Ferrarella's crossline miniseries, THE MOM SQUAD, with *Beauty and the Baby* (#1668), about widowed mother-to-be Lori O'Neill and the forbidden feelings she can't deny for her late husband's caring brother!

In Raye Morgan's *Betrothed to the Prince* (#1667), the second in the exciting CATCHING THE CROWN miniseries, a princess goes undercover when an abandoned baby is left in the care of a playboy prince. And some things are truly meant to be, as Carla Cassidy shows us in her incredibly tender SOULMATES series title, *A Gift from the Past* (#1669), about a couple given a surprising second chance at forever.

What happens when a rugged cowboy wins fifty million dollars? According to Debrah Morris, in *Tutoring Tucker* (#1670), he hires a sexy oil heiress to refine his rough-and-tumble ways, and they both get a lesson in love. Then two charity dating-game contestants get the shock of their lives when they discover *Oops...We're Married?* (#1671), by brand-new Silhouette Romance author Susan Lute.

See you next month for more fun-in-the-sun romances!

Happy reading!

Mary-Theresa Hussey

Mary-Theresa Hussey
Senior Editor

Please address questions and book requests to:
Silhouette Reader Service
U.S.: 3010 Walden Ave., P.O. Box 1325, Buffalo, NY 14269
Canadian: P.O. Box 609, Fort Erie, Ont. L2A 5X3

Beauty and the Baby

MARIE FERRARELLA

SILHOUETTE *Romance*®

Published by Silhouette Books

America's Publisher of Contemporary Romance

To single mothers everywhere,
struggling to make a difference in their children's lives.
I wish you strength and love.

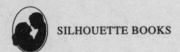 SILHOUETTE BOOKS

ISBN 0-373-19668-7

BEAUTY AND THE BABY

Copyright © 2003 by Marie Rydzynski-Ferrarella

Books by Marie Ferrarella in Miniseries

MARIE FERRARELLA

earned a master's degree in Shakespearean comedy, and, perhaps as a result, her writing is distinguished by humor and natural dialogue. This RITA® Award-winning author's goal is to entertain and to make people laugh and feel good. She has written over one hundred books for Silhouette, some under the name Marie Nicole. Her romances are beloved by fans worldwide and have been translated into Spanish, Italian, German, Russian, Polish, Japanese and Korean.

You'll enjoy
Marie Ferrarella's new miniseries,
The Mom Squad—four single mothers
who come together to experience
life's greatest miracle.

The MOM SQUAD

is…

Sherry Campbell—ambitious newswoman who
makes headlines when a handsome billionaire
arrives to sweep her off her feet…and shepherd
her new son into the world!
A Billionaire and a Baby, SE #1528, available
March 2003

Joanna Prescott—Nine months after her visit
to the sperm bank, her old love rescues her from
a burning house—then delivers her baby….
A Bachelor and a Baby, SD #1503, available
April 2003

Chris "C.J." Jones—FBI agent, expectant
mother and always on the case. When the baby
comes, will her irresistible partner be by her side?
The Baby Mission, IM #1220, available
May 2003

Lori O'Neill—A forbidden attraction blows
down this pregnant Lamaze teacher's tough-
woman facade and makes her consider the
love of a lifetime!
Beauty and the Baby, SR #1668, available
June2003

Chapter One

"You look tired," Carson O'Neill said.

Lifting her head, his sister-in-law smiled at him in response. Carson watched the dimples in both cheeks grow deeper. He wasn't a man who ordinarily noticed dimples. Involved in his work, he noticed very little these days.

But, in almost an unconscious way, he had become aware of a great many things about Lori O'Neill ever since fate and his late brother, Kurt, had sent the woman his way.

Ever since Carson could remember, he'd been a caretaker. It wasn't something he just decided to do one day, wasn't even something he admitted wanting to do. It was just something that needed doing, a hard fact of life. Like the way he'd looked after his mother after his father had left. And the way he'd always looked out for his younger brother. Or tried to.

And the way he'd wound up here, the director of

St. Augustine's Teen Center, a place that had too many kids and too little money, but was somehow— thanks to his all but superhuman efforts—still beating the odds and staying open.

Carson picked up a basketball that had whacked him against the back of his calves a second ago and tossed it toward a boy whose head barely came up to his chest. The boy flashed a sudden grin and ran off with his retrieved prize. As always, there was a game in progress.

His responsibilities weren't something he'd sought out. They'd just been there, waiting for him to walk in and take over. On his father's departure, his mother had all but become a basket case, so, at fifteen, Carson had become the family's driving force.

It wasn't easy. Kurt had been a screwup, albeit an incredibly charming one, and he'd loved Kurt, so he had done his best to help him out, to set him straight. Done his best to be there with silent support and not so silent money whenever the occasion had called for it. Which, as time progressed, was often.

Despite all Carson's efforts to set his brother on the right road, Kurt had managed to kill himself in his search for speed. ''Death by motorcycle,'' the newspaper had glibly reported on the last page in the section that dealt with local news.

Kurt's death, a year after his mother's, should have freed him from the role of patriarch, but it hadn't. There was Lori to think of. Somehow, it seemed only natural that he should take Kurt's pregnant wife under his wing.

Not that Lori had asked.

She was an independent, spirited woman, which was what he'd liked about her. But she was also pregnant and, after Kurt's untimely death, faced with a mountain of Kurt's debts.

The old adage, "When it rained, it poured," was never truer than in Lori's case. Less than a month after Kurt's death, the company for which Lori worked as a graphic artist declared bankruptcy, leaving her jobless. Carson found himself stepping in with both feet.

He'd stepped in the same way when he'd heard that the youth center, where he and Kurt had spent their adolescent afternoons, was about to close its doors because there was no one to take over as director and precious little financing.

His ex-wife, Jaclyn, had called him a bleeding heart when he'd told her he was leaving his law firm and taking over the helm at St. Augustine's Teen Center. He had discovered that being a lawyer left him cold and gave him no sense of satisfaction. Very quickly it had become just a means to an end. An end that had pleased Jaclyn a great deal, but not him. He'd needed more. He'd needed meaning.

The abrupt change in his life's direction had left her far from pleased. She had screamed at him, calling him a fool. Calling him a great many other things as well. He hadn't realized that she'd known those kinds of words until she'd hurled them at him.

The last label had been a surprise, though. She'd called him a bleeding heart. It showed how little, after five years of marriage, she really knew about him. He was pragmatic, not emotional. Taking over at the center had been something that needed doing, for so many reasons.

Besides, his heart didn't bleed, it didn't feel anything at all. Especially not after Jaclyn had left, taking their two-year-old daughter with them. His heart only functioned. Just as he did.

Just as Lori did, he thought, looking at her now. Except that she did it with verve. He motioned her to his office just down the narrow hall beyond the gym. The girls, whose game Lori had been refereeing, watched her for a moment, then went on without her.

He closed the door behind Lori, then indicated the chair in front of his scarred desk, a desk that was a far cry from the expensive one he'd been sitting behind three years ago.

Ordinarily, Lori seemed tireless to him, almost undaunted by anything that life threw her way. The only time he'd ever seen her be anything other than upbeat was at Kurt's funeral.

But even then, she'd seemed more interested in comforting him. Not that he'd allowed that, of course. He was his own person, his own fortress. It was the way it had always been and the way it would always be. He was who he was. A loner. Carson knew he couldn't be any other way even if he wanted to. Which he didn't.

"What?" Lori finally pressed.

She tried to read her brother-in-law's expression and failed. Nothing new there. Carson had always seemed inscrutable. Not like Kurt. She could always tell what Kurt was thinking if she looked into his eyes for more than a moment. Usually, he was trying to hide something.

"I've been watching you," Carson told her. "You seem tired today," he repeated.

Lori shook her head, denying the observation. She prided herself on being able to soldier on, no matter what. These days, however, the weight of her backpack was steadily increasing. Especially since she was carrying it in front of her.

"No, I'm not tired. Just a wee bit overwhelmed by all that energy out there." She nodded toward the area right outside the closetlike room that served as the youth center's general office. There were a few small rooms around the perimeter, but the center's main focus was the gym. It was there that the kids who frequented the center worked out their aggression and their tension.

Then, with a sigh, she slowly lowered herself into the chair in front of his desk, trying not to think about the daunting task of getting up again. She'd face that in a minute or so. Right now, it felt really good to be able to sit down.

Maybe she was tired at that, Lori thought. But she didn't like the idea that she showed it.

Just beyond the door were the sounds of kids letting off steam, channeling energy into something productive instead of destructive. Kids who, but for Carson's concentrated efforts, would have no place to go except into trouble.

She looked at her brother-in-law with affection. Carson had given up the promise of a lucrative life so that others could have a shot at having a decent one. Lori knew that these kids, every one of them, could have been Kurt or Carson all those years ago. Her late husband had told her all about his younger years on their second date, giving her details that had chilled her heart. Life had been hard here.

Both brothers had managed to come a long way from these mean streets, although it was easy enough for her to see that Kurt's soul had been anchored in the quick, the easy, the sleight of hand that arose from living the kinds of lives that were an everyday reality for the kids who came to St. Augustine's Youth Center. In a way, Kurt had never left that wild boy behind. It was that wild boy, she thought, that had eventually killed her husband.

Carson was another matter. Levelheaded, steadfast, Carson had chosen to walk on the straight and narrow safe side. He'd worked hard, put himself through school as he took care of his younger brother and mother. A football scholarship had helped. He'd believed his destiny lay with becoming a lawyer. He'd worked even harder once he'd graduated. A prestigious law firm had offered him a position and in exchange, he gave the firm his all.

Until three years ago. Thirty-eight months to be exact. That was when her brother-in-law had made the most selfless sacrifice she'd ever witnessed. He'd left the firm he'd been with to take on the headaches of the youth center that had been his salvation. But it hadn't been without a price.

Carson had taken on burdens and lost a wife.

Kurt had been against the move. He'd told his older brother that leaving the firm was the dumbest thing a grown man could do. All of his life, he'd struggled to get them both away from this very neighborhood and now he was returning to it. Embracing it at a great personal and financial cost.

It had made no sense to Kurt. But then, Kurt didn't understand what it meant to sacrifice. He'd never been that selfless. That had always been Carson's department.

And Carson was Carson, steadfast once he made a decision, unmoved by arguments, pleas or taunts, all of which had come from his wife before she'd packed up and left with their two-year-old daughter. Leaving him with divorce papers.

Lori knew losing his little girl had been what had hit Carson the hardest, although you'd never know it by anything that was ever said. But then, ever since she'd met him, Carson had always played everything close to the vest.

It was a wonder his chest wasn't crushed in by the weight, she mused now, looking at him. His desk was piled high with paperwork, which he hated. The man took a lot on himself. Would have taken her on as well if she'd allowed it. Again, that was just his way.

But she wasn't about to become another one of his burdens. She was a person, not a helpless rag doll. After Kurt's death, she'd squared her shoulders and forced herself to push on. To persevere. There were plenty of single mothers out there. She'd just joined the ranks, that was all. She'd taken this job only after Carson proved to her that it hadn't been offered out of charity, but because he really needed someone to help him out. It wasn't the kind of work she was used to, but it and the Lamaze classes she taught helped pay the bills. And they would do until something better came along.

Lori reasoned that as long as she kept good thoughts, eventually something better *had* to come along.

"You're also more than a little pregnant," Carson pointed out. The sun was shining into the room. There were telltale circles beneath her eyes. She wasn't getting enough sleep, he thought. "Maybe you should take it easier on yourself. Go home, Lori."

But she shook her head. "Can't. Rhonda didn't show up today, remember?"

He frowned. Rhonda Adams was one of the assistants who helped out at the center. Rhonda hadn't been showing up a lot lately. Something else he had to look into. Trouble was, finding someone to work long hours for little pay wasn't the easiest thing in the world.

"That's my concern," he told Lori, "not yours."

She hated the way he could turn a phrase and shut her out. She wondered if he did it intentionally, or if he was just oblivious to the effect of his words. "It is while you sign my paychecks."

"I don't sign your paychecks, the foundation does," he corrected. Foundation money and donations were what kept the teen center going, but times had gotten very tight.

Her eyes met his. He wasn't about to brush her off. "Figure of speech, Counselor."

"Don't call me that, I'm not a lawyer anymore."

Maybe he was getting a little too crabby these days. And he wasn't even sure why. Carson backed off.

She looked at him pointedly. "Then stop sounding like one."

"I'm serious, Lori. Don't tire yourself out. You are pregnant, even if you don't look it." His eyes swept over her form. Petite, the pert blue-eyed blonde was small-boned and if you looked quickly, her slightly rounded shape looked to be a trick played by some wayward breeze that had sneaked into the drafty gymnasium and had snuggled in beneath her blouse, billowing it out.

Lori looked down at her stomach. She'd felt pregnant from what she judged was the very first moment of conception. Somehow, she'd known, just known that there was something different that set this time apart from all the other times she and Kurt had made love.

Carson's words to the contrary, she felt huge. "Thanks," she quipped. "But right now, I feel as if I look like I'm smuggling a Thanksgiving turkey out of the building."

His mouth curved ever so slightly. "Looks to me like there's going to be a lot of people going hungry at that Thanksgiving dinner," he commented. He looked at her stomach again, trying to remember. "You're what, seven months along?"

"Eight, but who's counting?" she murmured.

She was, Lori added silently. Counting down every moment between now and her delivery date, fervently wishing that there was more time. More time in which to get ready for this colossal change that was coming into her life.

No one talking to her would have guessed at her true feelings. She was determined to keep up a brave front. She had to because of the Lamaze classes she taught at Blair Memorial Hospital twice a week. The women who attended them all looked to her as a calming influence, especially the three single moms-to-be with whom she'd bonded. She smiled to herself. If the women she was instructing only knew that her nerves were doing a frenzied dance inside of her every time she thought of the pending arrival, they wouldn't find her influence so calming.

She missed seeing the three women who had made up the group she'd whimsically dubbed The Mom Squad. But C.J., Joanna and Sherry's due dates were now in the past. The three all had beautiful, healthy babies now, and, by an odd turn of events, they also now had men at their sides who loved them. Men who wanted to spend the rest of their lives with them.

All she had were Kurt's pile of debts, which were dwindling thanks to her own tireless efforts, but none too quickly.

Stop feeling sorry for yourself, Lori upbraided herself. *You also have Carson.*

She glanced at the man who looked like a sterner, older version of her late husband. She wasn't about to minimize the effect of having him in her life. Having her brother-in-law's support went a long way toward helping her get her world in order.

Not that she leaned on him—well, not so that he really noticed. But just knowing he was around if she needed him meant a great deal to her. Carson had offered her a job helping at the center when her company had left her almost as high and dry as Kurt's death had. And he'd also been instrumental in pulling strings and getting her the job teaching the Lamaze classes at Blair.

That and the freelance work she found as a graphic designer helped her make ends meet. More importantly, it kept her sane. Kept her grief at bay. Kurt had never been a steady, dependable man, but in her own way, she'd loved him a great deal. Forgiven him a great deal, even his inability to grow up and take on responsibilities. Even the dalliances she'd discovered. It had taken her time, though, to forgive him his death.

She was still working on it.

Kurt had had no business racing like that, no business wanting to shake his fist at death just one more time because it made himself feel more powerful. Not when he had her and a baby on the way.

She sighed quietly. That had been Kurt—thoughtless, but engaging. At times, though, it had worn a little thin.

"Eight?" Carson echoed.

She looked at him, her thoughts dissipating. Carson had forgotten, she thought. But then, there were a lot more important things on his mind than her pregnancy. Like constantly searching for funding.

"You're that far along?"

She tried not to laugh at his incredulous expression. "You make it sound like a terminal disease."

Broad shoulders rose and fell in a vague fashion.

"I guess I just didn't realize…" An idea came to him suddenly. "I can have you placed on disability—" He didn't know where he'd find the money, but something could be arranged.

Lori knew what he was trying to do. Contrary to her ex-sister-in-law's beliefs, Carson's heart was in the right place, but in her book, what he was proposing was nothing short of charity.

"I'm not disabled," she countered.

He heard the stubborn tone in her voice. Admirable though her independence was, there were times when his sister-in-law could be a mule. Like now. "Yeah, I know, but technically maternity leave doesn't start until after you give birth."

It was her turn to shrug. "So, I'll stick around until I give birth."

"You should be home, Lori, taking care of yourself."

Carson didn't see what the problem was, or why she had him fighting a war on two fronts, one to get her a paid leave and one to get her to actually leave. When Jaclyn had been pregnant, she'd insisted on having a woman come in and do all the chores that she didn't normally do anyway. After Sandy was born, Hannah had stayed on to care for the house and the baby.

Jaclyn had always maintained that she was too delicate to put up with the drudgery of routine. He'd indulged her because he'd loved her and because she was his wife, his responsibility.

And because he'd been crazy about their child.

In hindsight, Hannah had taken care of Sandy better than Jaclyn ever could. Carson didn't mind paying for that. There was nothing too good for Sandy.

"I am taking care of myself," Lori insisted. She was accustomed to looking after herself. She'd been on her own since she was twenty. Even after she'd met Kurt, she'd been the one to take care of him, not the other way around. "If I stayed at home with my feet up, I'd go crazy inside of a week. Three days, probably." She smiled at Carson, appreciating his concern but determined not to let him boss her around. "Haven't you heard, Counselor? Work is therapeutic. Speaking of which, I'd better be getting back. There's a basketball game I'm supposed to be refereeing."

Bracing herself, she placed a hand on either wooden armrest and pushed herself up. The movement was a little too sudden, a little too fast. Lori's head started to spin.

The walls darkened. The small room began to close in on her.

A tiny pinprick of panic scratched her skin.

Lori struggled against the encroaching darkness, struggled to push the walls back out again. The effort was futile. The walls turned all black as they raced toward her with a frightening speed.

Perspiration beaded along her forehead.

And then there was nothing.

The next thing Lori knew, she felt herself being jerked up. Someone's arms were closing around her. There was heat everywhere, swirling about her.

She realized her eyes were shut.

With a mighty effort, she pushed them open again

and found herself looking up into Carson's dark blue, solemn eyes. They were darker than Kurt's eyes had been. And far more serious.

Lori tried to smile. Even that took effort. He was holding her. Holding her very close. Was that why it felt so hot all of a sudden?

Because he looked so concerned, she forced herself to sound light. "Didn't your mother ever tell you that if you scowl so hard, your face'll freeze that way?"

"My mother told me very little," he told her, his voice monotone.

She'd given him one hell of a scare, fainting like that. He had no idea what to think, what to do, other than to feel utterly helpless. Somebody needed to hand out instruction booklets when it came to women. Maybe even an entire desk encyclopedia.

Carson carried her over to the sagging, rust-colored leather sofa and placed her down as gently as he could manage.

His brow furrowed as he looked at her. "You want me to call a doctor?"

She caught hold of Carson's hand in case he had any ideas about acting on his question. "No, I want you to stop looking as if I'm about to explode any second."

His eyes were drawn to the small bump in her abdomen that represented his future niece or nephew. It was easy to forget Lori was pregnant at times. She looked so small. How could there be another human being inside of her?

Still, eight months was eight months. "Well, aren't you?"

She placed her other hand protectively over her abdomen. She could feel her baby moving. It always created a feeling of awe within her. Three months of kicking and shifting and she still hadn't gotten used to the sensation.

"No," she assured him, using the same tranquil, patient voice she used in the Lamaze classes, "not at the moment. Pregnant women faint, Carson." She used his hand to draw herself up into a sitting position. And then slowly to her feet. He hovered protectively around her. "It's one of the few pleasures left to them." Her smile was meant to put him at ease. "Don't worry about it."

His arm was around her, just in case her knees failed again. "Why do you have to be so damn stubborn?"

She flashed a grin at him. "Maybe that's what keeps me going."

He knew her well enough to know there was no winning. "At least let me drive you home."

Lori shook her head. "I brought my car."

"So?" Carson didn't see the problem. "I'll drive that."

She cocked her head, looking at him. The man was a dear. "Then how will you get back?"

He bit back an oath. "Do you have to overthink everything?"

"Can't help it." Her eyes sparkled as she smiled more broadly at him. "Must be the company I keep." She took a deep cleansing breath, then released it slowly, just as she'd demonstrated countless times in class. "There, all better. Really." But as she tried to walk away, she found that he was still holding her. Still unwilling to allow her to leave on her own power.

She was standing less than an inch away from him. Feeling things she didn't think that women in her condition were capable of feeling. At least not about men who weren't responsible for getting them into this condition in the first place.

Chapter Two

Lori looked down at her brother-in-law's hands. Strong, capable, and right now they were on either side of her arms, anchoring her in place. She raised her eyes to meet his.

"Um, Carson."

"What?" Impatience laced with annoyance framed the single word.

She gave a slight tug. "I can't go anywhere if you're still holding on to me."

By all rights, he knew he should drop his hands to his sides. She was a grown woman, more than capable of making her own decisions. He'd always believed in live and let live. At least on paper. But there were times when he felt she was being unnecessarily stubborn on principle.

"Maybe that's the idea," he told her.

"Eventually, one of us is going to have to go to the bathroom," she deadpanned. She glanced at her belly before looking up at him again. "Because of my condition, my guess is that it'll probably be me." A glimmer of a smile began to play on her lips. "I'd rather not have to ask for permission."

Carson felt a trace of embarrassment and wasn't sure if it was for her or himself. In either case, Carson dropped his hands in exasperation. But not before issuing a warning.

"First sign of you fading, I'm taking you home, no matter what you say." His eyes did almost as good a job as his hands at pinning her to the spot. "I'll be watching you."

"I never doubted it for a moment." The smile on her lips widened, reaching up to her eyes. He tried not to notice and failed miserably. There was something about Lori's eyes that always got to him. They had been the first thing he'd noticed about her when they'd met. The killer figure had been the second.

"What?" he finally bit off.

Surly on the outside, mushy on the inside, she thought fondly. "I just never envisioned my guardian angel would look like a football player, that's all."

Carson laughed shortly, his expression never changing. He'd been accused of being a lot of things in his time, but never an angel. Not even by his mother. Certainly not by his ex-wife.

"Got a hell of a long way to go before I'm anyone's guardian angel."

There was something in his eyes for a fleeting moment. Sadness? It was gone the next, but it succeeded in moving her. Carson didn't like being touched. Because she was a toucher and firmly believed in the benefits of human contact, she patted his cheek anyway. The man had been there for her, awkward, but ready to help right from the start. She wasn't about to forget that.

"Not nearly as far as you think, Carson." She turned on her heel with more ease than he thought possible for a woman in her condition. "Gotta get back to work."

But just as she stepped out the door, a dark-haired young woman swung open the door to the rear entrance and came rushing down the hall. In her haste, she narrowly avoided a collision with Lori.

Eyes the color of milk chocolate widened as the woman came to an abrupt halt less than an inch shy of impact. She sucked in her breath.

"Wow, sorry about that." She patted Lori's stomach. "Could have had an early delivery, huh?"

Carson's arm had closed protectively around Lori, pulling her back just in time. He glared at the other woman. Good help was hard to find. It was even harder to get it to come in on time. "There wouldn't have been any danger of that if you'd come in at ten the way you were supposed to, Rhonda."

The woman, barely three years out of her own teens and in Carson's opinion not yet fully entrenched in the adult world, gave him a high-wattage, apologetic grin. "Sorry, boss. Chuck decided to have a temper tantrum this morning."

Carson's frown deepened. His aide's current flame reminded him a lot of Kurt. "Either tell your boyfriend to grow up, or get another boyfriend."

His words rolled off her back like an inconsequential Southern California summer rain.

"Sorry," she repeated. "You don't pay me enough for that."

From what he knew, Rhonda was allowing her boyfriend to crash on her sofa. Chuck was currently "in between jobs," a place the man had been residing in from the time Carson had hired Rhonda. "Won't have to if the next boyfriend could hang onto a job."

The familiar words made him stop abruptly. He slanted a look at Lori, wondering if his exchange with Rhonda had scraped over any old wounds. He'd lectured Kurt about hanging on to a job more times than he could remember, especially after he'd married Lori. Kurt's response had always been to laugh off his words, as if he thought his older brother was joking. Kurt had maintained that he was still looking for his niche. As far as Carson knew, Kurt never found it.

"So he could be an old grump like you, boss man? Don't think so." Rhonda winked broadly at Carson, shoving her hands into the back pockets of her worn jeans. "I'd love to stand around and talk like this, but some of us have work to do." She waved to one of the young teens and hurried across the gym.

Carson turned his attention back to Lori. "There goes your excuse."

Lori looked at him. "You've lost me."

Interesting choice of words, he thought. And very appropriate.

"Just what I'm trying to do. At least for the rest of the afternoon. Rhonda can handle the kids." He nodded in the direction of the front entrance. "Go home and take a nap before class tonight."

It surprised her that he remembered her schedule, but then, she supposed it shouldn't. Carson liked to keep tabs on everything. It felt confining to her at times, but he never realized it. She knew he meant no harm.

She pressed her lips together, debating. It wouldn't hurt to grab a few minutes of her own, she thought. She'd been up half the night working on a new Web design project that had come in. When opportunity knocked, she couldn't afford not to be home. "You're not going to be satisfied until I go, are you?"

"Nope."

"Okay, you win." She sighed, surrendering. "Always like to keep the boss happy."

Carson crossed his arms before his rock-solid chest. "Right, and I'm the bluebird of happiness."

Her eyes swept over him. He was still every inch the football player who'd made the winning touchdown in the last game he ever played. "I wouldn't perch on any branches if I were you."

He grumbled something not entirely under his breath. Laughing, Lori walked away, heading for the lockers on the other end of the first floor. She was very conscious of his watching her and tried very hard not to move from side to side the way she felt inclined to these days. Or to place a hand to the small of her back in order to ease the ache there. Pregnant women did that and Carson seemed to equate pregnancy with weakness. The more she fit his stereotype, the more determined he would be to try to convince her to stay home.

She wasn't the stay-at-home type.

Lori made her way to the shadowy row of lockers where the kids stashed their backpacks, books and various paraphernalia while they used the facilities. Once out of eye range, she pressed her hand to the small of her back and massaged for a moment. For a peanut, this baby was giving her some backache.

After stretching, she went to her locker. Wanting to seem more like one of the teens, Lori had taken a locker to store her own belongings there. Usually, she only had her purse.

She paused in front of the upper locker, trying to remember her combination. It was nestled in over-crowded memory banks that retained every number that had any bearing on her life. She seemed to retain all manner of numbers, not just her own social security number, but her late husband's as well. It was in there with her license plate and the phone numbers and birthdays of several dozen people who currently figured prominently in her life.

She smiled as the combination came to her. Turning the dial on the old lock three revolutions to the left, a muffled sound caught her attention. Lori stopped and listened.

The sound came again.

It was a sob, she was sure of it. The kind that was muted by hands being pressed helplessly over a mouth too distressed to seal away the noise.

Concerned, curious, Lori set the lock back against

the metal door and moved around to the other side of the bank of battered lockers.

Huddled in the corner, her long tanned legs pulled in tightly against her chest, was one of the girls she'd missed seeing today. The young girl sounded as if her heart was breaking. Boy trouble?

"Angela?"

The girl only pulled herself in tighter. Someone else might have felt as if they were intruding and left. Lori's mind had never worked that way. Anyone in pain needed to be soothed.

She took a few steps toward the girl. "Angela, what's wrong?"

"Nothin'." The girl jerked her head up, wiping away the tears from her cheeks with the heel of her hand. She tossed her head defiantly, looking away. Her silence told Lori that this was none of her business.

Lori chose not to hear.

For her, working at the center was a complete departure from life as she had known it. Here the word "deprived" didn't mean not having the latest video game as soon as it came out. "Doing without" had serious connotations here that involved ill-fitting hand-me-down clothing and hunger pangs that had nothing to do with dieting. Here, life was painted in bleaker colors.

But then, that was what the center was for, painting rainbows over the shades of gray.

"Sorry, but I think it's something." Angela kept her face averted. "The tears were a dead giveaway." Still nothing. "You know, for a pregnant woman, I can be very patient." Lori planted herself in front of the teenager. "I'm not going away until you level with me and tell me why you're sitting here by yourself, watering your knees."

Normally, her banter could evoke a smile out of the girl. But not today.

This was worse than she thought. With effort, Lori lowered herself to the girl's level. Her voice lost its teasing banter. "C'mon, Angela. Talk to me. Maybe I can help."

Angela shook her head. Fresh tears formed in the corners of her eyes. "Nobody can help me." She sighed with a hopelessness that was far too old for her to be feeling. "Except maybe a doctor."

In that moment, Lori understood. She knew what had reduced the fifteen-year-old to this kind of despair and tears.

Lori placed her hand on the girl's shoulder. She was so thin, so small. And living a nightmare shared by so many.

"Are you in trouble, Angela?"

It was an old-fashioned term, Lori knew, but in its own way as appropriate today as it had been when it was first coined. Because a pregnant girl just barely in high school was most assuredly in trouble.

The sigh was bottomless. "Yeah, I'll say." She sniffled. Lori dug into her pocket and pulled out a tissue, offering it to her. Angela took it and dried the fresh tears. Her voice quavered as she spoke. "A hell of a lot of trouble."

There were no indications that the girl was pregnant, but then, she hadn't looked it herself until just recently, Lori thought. "How far along are you?"

"I don't know." Angela shrugged restlessly. She looked down at the tissue. It was shredding. "It's been over two months, I think."

"You need to see a doctor."

Lori could see the beginning of a new thought entering the girl's eyes. "Yeah, somebody who can make this go away."

Lori shook her head. She didn't want Angela thinking that she was cavalierly suggesting she have an abortion. Decisions like that couldn't be made quickly.

"No. Somebody who can tell you what's going on with your body." She took the girl's hands into her own, forming a bond. "You might not be pregnant, it might be something else." Although, Lori thought, other possibilities could be equally as frightening to a fifteen-year-old as having a baby.

Thin, dark brown brows furrowed in confusion as Angela looked at her. "Like what?"

She didn't know enough about medicine to hypothesize. "That's what you need to find out. Do you have a doctor?"

Again the thin shoulders rose and fell, half vague, half defiant. "There's this doctor on Figueroa Street. I hear she's pretty decent."

Lori thought of her own doctor, a woman she'd been going to and trusted since she'd gotten out of college. Dr. Sheila Pollack had become more like a friend than just a physician. Angela needed someone like that right now, a professional who could clear up the mysteries for her and keep her healthy. Someone who could make her feel at ease rather than afraid.

"All right, go to her."

Angela frowned. "Word on the street is she don't do no abortions."

The girl's mind was stuck in a groove that might not be the answer she needed, or would even want a few months down the line. "Don't do anything hasty," Lori counseled. "If you're pregnant, talk to your mother."

Angela looked at her as if she'd just suggested she cover herself with honey and walk into cave full of bears. "Yeah, right and have her kill me? No thanks." There was disdain in the teen's voice, as if she'd just lost all credibility in the young girl's eyes.

When she moved to put her arm around the girl's shoulders, Angela jerked away. Lori wasn't put off. She tried again, more firmly this time. Angela needed to get a few barriers down. "She might surprise you."

Angela blew out a mocking breath. "Only surprises my mother gives me are the boyfriends she brings home." She shivered.

Had one of them put the moves on Angela? It wouldn't have been the first time in history something like that had happened. Lori tread carefully, determined to do the right thing and not fail this girl she hadn't known six months ago.

"If you want, I can talk to your mother for you."

Angela buried her face in her hands. Lori sat beside her on the floor, stroking her hair. "What I want is not to be pregnant."

"First find out if you are pregnant."

Angela slowly raised her head and looked at her. "And then?"

"And then—" With effort, Lori raised herself to her feet, "—we'll go from there. One step at a time. When I see you tomorrow, Angela, I want you to tell me you have an appointment with the doctor."

The girl nodded, scrambled up to her feet and wiped away the last of the telltale streaks from her face. She looked at her for a long moment. And then, slowly, just the barest of smiles emerged. "You know, you're pretty pushy for a pregnant woman."

"You're not the first one to tell me that." Lori slipped her arm around the girl's shoulder and gave her a quick hug.

She couldn't get Angela's face out of her mind. All through her instructions at the Lamaze class, Lori kept visualizing Angela in her mind's eye. She could almost see her here at Blair, taking classes to prepare for the monumental change that lay ahead of her.

The classes weren't enough, Lori thought. Not for her and certainly not for a fifteen-year-old.

The classes Lori gave with such authority taught woman how to give birth, but not what to do after that. Not really, not if she was being honest with herself. There was more to being a parent than knowing how to give a sponge bath to a newborn and that you should support their heads above all else. So much more.

Lori walked down the long, brightly lit corridor of the first floor of one of Blair Memorial's annex buildings. She'd waited until the last couple had left before locking up. The building felt lonely to her despite the bright lights. Seeing Angela huddled in a corner like that today had brought out all her own insecurities and fears. She had no mother to cower before, but there wasn't a mother to turn to for guidance, either.

She missed her mother, Lori thought not for the first time as she unlocked the door of her 1995 Honda Civic. Missed her something awful. For once, she lowered her defenses and allowed the sadness to come.

With a sigh, she started up her car. Leukemia had robbed her of her mother more than a dozen years ago. A heart attack had claimed her father just as she was in the middle of college. By twenty, she was all alone and struggling to make the best of it. And then Kurt had entered her life and she felt as if the sun had finally come out in her world.

Now here she was, eight years later, struggling all over again. The upbeat, feisty manner that the rest of the world saw was not always a hundred percent authentic. There were times which she really ached to have someone in her corner.

She had someone in her corner, Lori reminded herself as she turned down the hospital's winding path. She had Carson.

Leaving the hospital grounds, she fleetingly debated stopping by the old-fashioned Ice Cream Parlor where she and the other three single mothers had so often gone after classes, eager to temporarily drown their problems in creamy confections sinfully overloaded with whipped cream and empty, sumptuous calories.

It wasn't nearly as much fun alone.

Lori drove by the establishment. It was still open and doing a brisk business. The tables beside the bay windows were all filled. She wavered only for a moment before she pressed down on the gas pedal. The Ice Cream Parlor became a reflection in her rearview mirror.

She couldn't help wondering what the other women were doing tonight and if they still found motherhood as exciting as they had in the beginning.

Would she? Or was her only certainty these days the fact that she found the prospect of giving birth and motherhood scary as hell?

She came to a stop at a red light. Her hands felt slippery on the steering wheel.

Opening night jitters, she told herself.

Her due date was breathing down her neck and although part of her felt as if she had been pregnant since the beginning of time, another part of her did not want to race to the finish line, did not want the awesome weight of being responsible for the welfare of someone else other than herself.

"I know what you're going through, Angela," she whispered into the darkness as she eased onto the gas pedal again.

Right now, Angela probably felt isolated and alone. Maybe if she gave the girl a call, to see how she was doing and if she'd called to make an appointment with the doctor, Angela wouldn't feel so alone.

The next moment, the thought was shot down in flames. She didn't have Angela's number. On top of that, she wasn't even sure where the girl lived or what her mother's name was, so surfing through the Internet's numerous helpful sites wouldn't be productive.

The number, she realized, was probably on Carson's computer.

Lori made a U-turn at the end of the next block and pointed her vehicle back toward the center.

By car, St. Augustine's Teen Center was only fifteen minutes away from Bedford and home, but it might as well have resided in a completely different world. Here, the streets were narrow rather than wide, and the neighborhoods had not grown old gracefully. The windows of the buildings seemed to be staring out hopelessly at cars as they drove by. The street lights cast shadows rather than illumination. It made Lori sad just to be here.

This was the kind of neighborhood Kurt and Carson had grown up in, she thought. The kind they had both tried to leave behind.

Except that Carson had come back. By choice.

Lori saw St. Augustine's Teen Center up ahead. Lights came from the rear of the building where Carson kept his office. She glanced at her watch. It was past eight.

What was Carson still doing here?

Chapter Three

The parking lot was deserted, except for Carson's beat-up pickup truck. His other car, a sedan, was housed in his garage at home. Right beside the classic Buick Skylark he had been lovingly restoring for the past three years. Lori had a hunch that working on the car was what kept him sane.

Everyone needed something, she mused.

Parking beside the truck, Lori got out and crossed to the rear entrance. Curiosity piqued, she let herself into the building and walked down the short hallway to the back office. Light was pooling out into the room onto the floor outside, beckoning to her.

For a moment, she stood in the doorway, watching him, trying to be impartial. Carson was really a very good-looking man, she thought. Handsomer, actually, than Kurt had been. There was a maturity about him, a steadfastness that marked his features. It was a plateau that Kurt hadn't reached yet.

What Carson needed, she decided, was a life. A life that went beyond these trouble-filled walls. Contrast was always a good thing.

Right now, he looked like a man with the weight of the world on his shoulders. A weight he guarded jealously. Carson O'Neill wasn't a man who shared responsibility or had ever learned how to delegate. He thought he had to do it all in order for it to be done right.

Carson glanced up. He'd thought he felt someone looking at him, but he hadn't expected it to be Lori. If he was surprised to see her standing there, he made sure he didn't show it. He let the papers he was shuffling through sit quietly on the desk.

"Can't seem to get rid of you, can I?" And then he realized how late it was. How did she get in after hours? It was late. "I thought I locked up."

"You did. I have keys, remember?" She held them up and jingled the set for his benefit before slipping them back into her purse.

He laughed shortly. "That'll teach me to hand out keys indiscriminately."

"You really are in a mood tonight, aren't you?" She noted that he wasn't smiling and there was an edge to his words.

Carson laced his fingers together as he leaned back in his chair and rocked, looking at the stack of bills that never seemed to go away, never seemed to get smaller. It felt as if he had come full circle in his life, except that this time, he was hunting for funds at work instead of in his private life.

"Looking for money that isn't there always does that to me."

She crossed to his desk and picked up the last paper in his in-box. It was from the electric company. The one beneath it was for the phones. Both were past due. She had a feeling they weren't the only ones.

Dropping the papers, Lori raised her eyes to his. "Trouble keeping the wolf away from the door?"

He shook his head. Times were tight. People picked and chose their charities carefully. St. Augustine's had no name and wasn't at the top of anyone's list. If it closed its doors, no one would notice. No one except the kids who needed it most.

Carson sighed. "It's beyond trouble. More like a major disaster." He glanced at the figures on the computer monitor again. They didn't get any better no matter how many times he looked at them. "I'm trying to meet 2003 prices with a 1950s budget."

Her heart went out to him. He was one of the good guys no matter what kind of face he tried to present to the world. But she was a firm believer in it always being darkest before the dawn. Somehow, he'd find the money to make it through one more month. And then another, and another. He had before.

Lori smiled at him. "I think this is the part where Mickey Rooney jumps up on a table and shouts, 'Hey kids, let's save the old place by putting on a show.'"

The funny thing was, Carson understood what she was talking about. She'd made him watch one of those old movies once. It was while Kurt was still alive. His brother was out of town on some get-rich-quick venture and he'd come down with the flu. This was right after he'd taken over at the center and Jaclyn had walked out on him. Lori had come by with chicken soup she'd made from scratch and a sack of videotapes to entertain him despite his protests to the contrary. It was around then that he'd begun to seriously envy his brother.

But he scowled now. He needed a miracle, not an old movie grounded in fantasy. "People really watched films like that in the old days?"

She nodded. "Ate them up."

He pushed himself away from the desk, wishing he could push himself away from the bills as easily. "Well, there's no one to put on a show here."

Lori had felt tired until she'd walked in. Now, one thought was forming into one hell of an idea. "No, but there could be a fund-raiser."

"What?" She was babbling, he thought. Fund-raisers were for fashionable causes backed by wealthy foundations and people blessed with too much money and too much time on their hands.

Lori's mind was racing. There was Sherry's fiancé, not to mention the man who had returned into Joanna's life. Both were well-connected billionaires in their own right. It could work.

Her grin was almost blinding. It matched the sparkle in her eyes as she turned them on him. He had trouble keeping his mind on the situation.

"I know a few people who know a few people who have more money than God." Maybe it was time she got together with the ladies of the Mom Squad again, Lori thought. She'd been the one who had baptized the group, the one who had been instrumental in bringing them all together for mutual support in the first place. Maybe it was time to spread some of that support around. "From what I hear, they're always up for worthy causes."

Even so, that did him no good. "And probably get hit up by them every other minute of their lives."

She looked at him fondly. No one would ever accuse Carson of being a rampaging optimist. "Which is why having the inside track is a good thing."

He looked at her skeptically. "And you have the inside track."

He didn't believe her. What else was new? She had a feeling that if he ever traced his family tree, he would find that his lineage went back to the original Doubting Thomas.

"Anymore 'inside,' she told him, "and it might have to be surgically removed."

"What the hell do they put in those prenatal vitamins of yours?" She was dreaming, pure and simple. And wasting his time with pipe dreams. Miracles didn't happen to people like him.

She'd made up her mind about this and she wasn't about to allow him to rain on her parade. "Energy."

He laughed, shaking his head. Watching her as she moved about his broom closet of an office. "Like you need some."

Her eyes laughed at him. The man was never satisfied. She'd be satisfied just removing the furrow from between his brows. "This afternoon you were complaining I looked tired." She grinned. "There is just no pleasing you, is there?"

She had a way of lighting up a room, he thought,

even when he wanted nothing else than to stay in the dark. "You don't have to please me, Lori—"

Lori came around to his side of the desk and then sat down on top of it. She looked down on Carson, her eyes teasing him. "No, but I'd like to try. It's a dirty job but someone has to do it."

"Why?"

His eyes looked so serious. Her grin softened into a smile. "Because you deserve to be happy."

He lifted his shoulders, shrugging carelessly. "Not according to my ex-wife."

"What does she know?" Lori scoffed. She'd never really liked Jaclyn. The woman had turned out to be a self-serving gold digger, pushing Carson to get further along in his career not for his benefit, but for hers. "If she knew anything, she wouldn't be your ex-wife, she'd still be your wife."

The assertion embarrassed him. He didn't know how to handle compliments. He never had. "What are you doing here, anyway?"

She'd almost forgotten. "I came to see if I could find Angela's phone number."

More than a hundred and seventy kids came to the center during the week. He was drawing a blank. "Angela?"

"The tall, thin girl who's so good at basketball. Brunette, dark brown eyes. Laughs like a blue jay," she prompted.

The last struck a chord. "Oh, right." And then he looked at her. He couldn't think of a more unlikely coupling. "Why do you want her number?"

She debated just how much she should tell him. "I want to see how she's doing."

"Why? Can't find anyone your own age to play with?" Carson studied her face in the dim light. "You're serious."

"Yes."

He couldn't read her expression any more than he could read Japanese. "Why would you want to see how she's doing?" Instincts told him not to drop the matter. "Something wrong?"

Lori didn't want to break a confidence. "It could be."

The expression on Carson's face told her she'd lost all chance of leaving the building with the phone number without giving him some sort of an explanation. She hadn't promised Angela not to tell anyone, but it had been implied. Still, Carson had a good heart, despite his tough, blustery manner and he'd been running this center for a while now. He had a right to know what was going on. Besides, he might be able to offer some insight into how to handle the situation.

Lori bit her lower lip. "She thinks she might be pregnant."

The news stunned him. He stared at Lori blankly, wondering if he'd heard right. "She's only, what, thirteen?"

"Fifteen," Lori corrected, although she could see how he'd make the mistake. Angela had a baby face that made her look younger than she was.

Thirteen, fifteen, there hardly seemed a difference. "A baby."

She knew how Carson felt. But it was a sad fact of life. "Babies have been having babies for a long time now."

Carson scrubbed his hand over his face. Damn it, the center was supposed to prevent this kind of thing. The kids were supposed to use up their energy on sports, not sex. "How do you figure into this?"

"I found her crying in the back of the locker area today and got her to talk to me."

Lori had that kind of knack, he thought, the kind that made people open up to her, even hard cases. At times even he had trouble keeping his own counsel around her. "Does her mother know?"

She shook her head. "I think Angela's afraid of her mother."

"I'd be afraid of my mother if I was pregnant at fifteen."

She laughed. "If you were pregnant at fifteen, it would have made all the scientific journals." Her grin broadened and she was relieved to be able to have something to laugh at. "If you were pregnant at any age, it would have made the scientific journals."

Carson gave her a dry look. "Very funny." Maybe it would do Angela some good to talk to Lori, he reasoned. Girls in trouble tended to do drastic things. Minimizing his current program, Carson typed in something on his keyboard and brought up a directory. He scrolled down the screen. "Here it is, Angela Coleman." Taking an index card, he jotted down the phone number for Lori, then handed it to her.

She looked at the single line, then held the card out to him. "How about the address?"

"Oh no, I don't want you driving there in your condition." When she turned to look at the screen, he shut the program.

She frowned at his screensaver. "The DMV have a ban on pregnant women?"

She was going to fight him on this, he just knew it. The woman didn't have the sense of a flea. "Lori, it's not the safest neighborhood." He shouldn't have to tell her that.

"Angela lives there."

There were times he just wanted to take Lori by the shoulders and shake her. Because there were times that her Pollyanna attitude could put her in serious jeopardy. It was bad enough that she traveled here to work. He didn't want her taking unnecessary chances by pressing her luck. "There's nothing I can do about that. There is something I can do about you, though."

She knew he meant well, but good intentions still didn't give him the right to order her around. "Slavery went out a hundred and thirty-seven years ago, Carson. You don't own me."

He rose from his chair and looked down at her. "No, but I'm bigger."

Lori wiggled off the desk. And met him toe to toe, raising her chin defiantly. "Plan to stuff me into a box?"

Damn but her chin did present a tempting target. So did her lips. The thought shook him and he blocked it almost immediately. But not soon enough to erase it or its effect on him.

"If I have to."

And then her expression softened. He couldn't tell

if she'd been putting him on or not. Or was doing so now. "In your own twisted little way, you care about me, don't you?"

"Don't overanalyze everything." He didn't want this going any further. "You're carrying around my niece or nephew in there, that gives me the right to tell you not to be an idiot."

"You do have a way with words." Lori looked at him for a long moment. Others might buy into his gruff routine, but she didn't. She'd seen something else in his eyes. A man who didn't know how to connect. Even though he sorely needed to. "You miss her a lot, don't you?"

Now what the hell was she talking about? It was getting late and he was in no mood for this. "Who?" he snapped.

"Sandy."

The mention of his now five-year-old daughter took some of the fire out of him. He let his guard down an inch. There was no shame in admitting his feelings about the little girl. "Don't get to see her nearly enough."

That was because he spent nearly every waking minute here, she thought. "Why don't you take tomorrow off? I'll cover for you. Go see your daughter."

It wasn't nearly that simple. "I've got limited visitation rights," he ground out.

She'd forgotten about that. He'd told her about it during the only time she had ever seen him intoxicated. The terms of the divorce had just been worked out. Jaclyn in her wrath had hit him where she knew it would hurt the most. She'd used their daughter as a tool to get back at him.

Lori felt badly about raising a sore point. "It's not fair, you know."

He shrugged. There was nothing he could do about that now. "Whoever said that life was fair?" Carson shut down the computer and closed the monitor. He nodded at the card she was still holding. "Well, you've got your phone number. C'mon, I'll walk you to your car."

Nodding, she turned toward the door. "Okay."

"What," he feigned surprise, "no argument?"

She stopped in the doorway. "I can muster up something if you really want me to."

Ushering her over the threshold, he locked the office door behind him. "Never mind."

"You leaving, too?" Even as she asked, she laced both her arms through his.

He tried not to notice how close she was. Or that he found it oddly comforting and unsettling at the same time. He told himself that he was too tired to think clearly about anything. "There's no squeezing blood out of a stone."

She waited as he first locked the rear entrance, then tested the door to make sure it wouldn't give. "You know, I meant what I said."

Turning from the door, he began to walk to the cars. He was careful to keep a little distance between them. The night air felt warm and balmy and for some reason, he didn't feel quite in control of the situation.

"About what? You said a lot of things. You always say a lot of things."

If he was trying to divert her attention, he wasn't succeeding, she thought. "About the fund-raiser."

It was against his grain to go begging with his hat in his hand. But this wasn't for him, it was for the center. Maybe that was the way to go. But he was too tired to think intelligently about it tonight. "We'll talk about it tomorrow."

She'd more than half expected him to turn her down flat. "Really?"

Why did she have to question everything? "I said it didn't I?"

Pleased at the victory and enthused about the possibilities that a true fund-raiser could open up, Lori threw her arms around his neck and kissed him.

It was only meant to be just a light little peck on the lips. That was the way it started.

But then the peck became something more.

The contact between their lips opened a door, allowing something to seep out that had been kept, unconsciously, tightly under wraps by both of them.

Something warm and volatile.

And demanding.

Surprised, Lori looked into his eyes as she pulled her mouth back. Exactly one second before she kissed him again, harder this time. And with a great deal more feeling.

He meant to stop her, he really did. This was his sister-in-law for heaven's sake. By no means was this kind of thing supposed to happen outside of the realm of the Old Testament where men were encouraged to marry their dead brothers' widows.

But the taste of her soft lips feverishly pressed

against his had aroused something within him. Had unearthed feelings that he would have sworn on a stack of Bibles had been all but ground out beneath the heel of his ex-wife's shoe as she'd walked out of his life.

Carson wasn't altogether certain about their demise anymore. Those feelings felt very much alive and well, beating their wings within his chest.

His hands slipped from Lori's shoulders to her back. For a mindless moment, he pressed her closer as the sweetness of her mouth filled him. Filled all the empty, gaping holes within his soul like water rushing into an abyss.

Carson could feel his blood pumping hard through his veins, reminding him that there was more to him than just someone who came in early, left late and spent the core of his day trying to make a difference in the lives of kids most of society didn't care about.

Reminding him that he was a man. A man with needs that had been long neglected.

She hadn't meant for her kiss to be anything but innocent. Maybe her exuberance had gone too far, taking her to a place she had no business being. But oh, it did feel good to kiss a man. To be kissed by a man as if she mattered.

She could feel her head spinning, could feel her pulse racing. Making her glad to be alive.

For a moment longer, Lori allowed herself to linger, to ride this wild, surprising wave that took her into regions which were at once thrilling and frightening. Frightening because she wasn't supposed to be feeling this way, wasn't supposed to be reacting this way.

She was more than eight months pregnant for heaven's sake.

It didn't matter. All that mattered was this kiss.

And this man.

And then she became aware of something else. The baby picked that moment to kick.

Carson felt the punt being delivered to his lower abdomen. Reality came flying back with it. What the hell was he doing? This was wrong, all wrong.

Lori felt his hands leaving the small of her back, felt them grip her shoulders again. Then felt the bitter-sweetness of separation. His eyes were dark when he looked into her face.

"I'm not Kurt."

She shouldn't have done that, she thought. Shouldn't have jeopardized their friendship this way.

"I know." She smiled at him, struggling for humor, for control. "He wasn't as tall as you." Lori rubbed the back of her neck. "You're giving me a crick in my neck, Carson."

Her words diminished the seriousness of the moment. Carson gravitated toward it like a drowning man to a lifeline.

What the hell was that, he silently demanded of himself. It was so out of the boundaries of their relationship that he could have easily sworn it hadn't happened.

Except that it had and he felt shaken down to his shoes.

"Sorry about that," he mumbled.

She didn't know if he was talking about the crick in her neck, or about the kiss that had overtaken both of them. She took a chance he meant the latter. "Don't be. I'm not."

The look in her eyes went clear down to the center of the soul he was certain he no longer possessed. "It's late. I'll follow you in my car."

She tried to read his expression. Even if the lighting was better, she had a feeling she'd fail. "Are you coming over?"

He was surprised at the question. "No, just to make sure you get home safely."

"I know how to drive, Carson. Pregnancy doesn't affect my ability to navigate."

If that was true, the last few seconds wouldn't have happened. "I wouldn't be so sure about that."

She shook her head. "You know, Carson, you'd be a very sweet man if you didn't get in your own way all the time."

He had no idea what that meant. He felt like a man scrambling for high ground. "I don't want to be a sweet man."

"Too late." She smiled up at him again, her expression doing strange things to his insides. "You can huff and puff all you want, Carson. But you don't fool me. I know the inner you."

"I thought your degree was in digital arts, not psychoanalysis."

"This isn't a football field, you don't have to bob and weave to avoid getting tackled." Her voice softened into a whisper. "I'm not trying to tackle you, Carson."

Maybe, he thought, but he didn't know what the hell she *was* trying to do. Or what the hell was wrong with him. He shouldn't have kissed her.

But she had been the one who had kissed him, he reminded himself.

All right, then, he shouldn't have kissed her back.

At a complete loss, he looked down at her as she opened her door and slid in behind the steering wheel.

"Go home, Carson. I can drive myself home without any mishaps."

As far as he was concerned, she'd already had one this evening. They both had.

Like a man frozen to the spot, Carson stood and watched his sister-in-law drive away. It was better than trying to sift through the jumble that served as his emotions.

Chapter Four

Poor Carson.

Lori felt her mouth curving as she took the freeway off-ramp onto Bedford's main thoroughfare. He'd looked absolutely stunned when he'd pulled away from her in the parking lot. She supposed she must have, too, though at least she knew that was how she'd felt.

Talk about surprises. She had no idea the man could kiss that way.

Had to be the best-kept secret around, she mused, since as far as she knew, her brother-in-law had no social life to speak of. Kurt had tried to fix him up a few times after his divorce but Carson had made it clear in no uncertain terms that he wasn't interested in dating again. Ever. He'd mumbled something about women being more trouble than they were worth. She'd begun to think of him as a hermit.

She could feel her smile broaden. And she'd

thought that Kurt was a fabulous kisser. She doubted that it was time dimming her memory of him, but her late husband had to take a back seat to his big brother.

Must run in the family. Maybe it was a genetic thing.

She turned down a long, oak-lined street. If the women in Bedford only knew what she knew now, the man would never know another quiet moment, she speculated.

Not that she was all that experienced when it came to male-female relationships, or even kissing. She couldn't exactly be accused of being a party girl— ever.

But she knew a lackluster kisser when she ran into one. Until Kurt had come into her life, she'd actually thought that the closeness thing was highly overrated. Until Kurt, no man had ever sent her head spinning and her pulse spiking off the charts the way some of her girlfriends liked to claim that their boyfriends did.

Kurt had been a wonderful lover. Kind, attentive, tender. It was why she could forgive his transgressions and shortcomings. In bed and out, her husband had been utterly engaging.

Impatient to get home now, she shifted restlessly in her seat, her seat belt chafing her, as she just missed catching the light. With a heavy sigh, she pushed down on the brake and waited. Traffic was sparse.

She wouldn't have thought that was something Kurt and his brother had in common. At least, not the kissing part. God knew the brothers O'Neill were both good-looking, tall, broad-shouldered, slim-hipped, with chiseled features that could set an Egyptian mummy's pulse going at ten paces. But there'd always been a spark in Kurt's light blue eyes. Even without saying a word, he had a way of making you feel that you were the only one in the room.

With Carson, you knew you were in the room but you weren't sure if he was. The man brought new meaning to the term strong, silent type.

Except that now, he brought a new meaning to the word "wow."

Lori ran her tongue along her lips before she realized what she was doing. She could still taste him. She felt a flutter in her stomach. The baby was trying to get comfortable again.

Stop it. He's your brother-in-law, not to mention your boss. Don't make anything out of this. It was a kiss, a plain, ordinary kiss. Just something that happened, that's all.

Maybe so, but she couldn't help wondering if perhaps, just perhaps, the sensual similarities between the brothers didn't end with just their lips. She seemed to have less control over her mind than over the earth's rotation on its axis.

Could Carson set sheets on fire like Kurt had?

No reason to believe that, and no way you're ever going to find out.

The warning echoed in her brain, causing reality to rush in again.

She was perfectly willing to believe that her condition was affecting her thought processes. That, and the fact that she was lonely.

Despite juggling portions of three jobs, despite her friends and her work at the center, despite the fact that almost every minute of her day outside the house was filled with noise, people and activity, Lori was lonely. Lonely for the intimate touch of a man's hand. Lonely for that sweet sense of sharing that was the very best part of a marriage.

Pulling up into her driveway, she all but yanked the emergency bake out of its socket as she brought the vehicle to a dead stop.

Get a grip, Lori, she cautioned herself.

As best she could, she snaked her way out from behind the wheel. She'd pushed the seat back as far as she could and still be able to reach the pedals. The space between her and the steering wheel still felt as if it was shrinking at an alarming rate. With each day that past, she felt more and more like a cork being wedged into the opening of bottle every time she got into the car. God, but she couldn't wait until she was herself again.

But then you'll have the baby to take care of.

The prospect of what was ahead of her once she gave birth was even scarier in the dark. She hoped this was just a phase she was going through.

Coming in, she closed the door behind her and kicked off her shoes. Lori dropped her purse on the floor beside them. The purse tipped over and two pens came rolling out. Not up to bending down, she left them there.

Someday, she thought, she was going to have to put a table next to the front door. But not tonight.

She felt tired and edgy at the same time.

She tried to tell herself it had to do with the baby, but she knew better. What she needed, she decided, was to get her mind off what had happened in the center's parking lot and onto something else. Something productive.

Lori took the phone number Carson had written down for her out of her pocket. The debate about whether or not she should make a call lasted only as long as it took her to walk to her phone in the living room. Picking up the cordless receiver, she crossed to the sofa and sank into a corner.

It wasn't possible to make herself comfortable. Pregnancy had taken that option away from her, but she made herself the least uncomfortable she could. Looking at the number on her lap, Lori pressed the area code and then the rest of the numbers that would connect her to Angela's house.

The phone rang nine times on the other end before anyone picked up. When they did, they sounded far from happy.

"Hello?" a woman's voice snapped.

She wondered if this was Angela's mother. She certainly didn't sound friendly. "May I speak to Angela, please?"

"She's not here."

There was no effort to take a message. Lori had a feeling the woman was going to hang up. She talked quickly. "When do you expect her back?"

The irritation level of the woman's voice rose a notch. "Who knows? Kid comes and goes."

Lori glanced at her watch. It was after nine. "But it's a school night."

"So? You her teacher?" the woman challenged.

"No."

The woman shot another question at her before she could elaborate. "The police?"

"No."

The next thing Lori knew, there was a dial tone buzzing in her ear. She sighed, pressing the off button on the phone's receiver. She stared at it for a moment, empathizing. No wonder Angela didn't feel she could talk to her mother.

But the girl could talk to her. Anytime. She had to impress that on Angela. And if Angela was pregnant, then Lori would go with her when she went to face her mother with the news. That Angela's mother had to be informed of her condition was not up for debate. The woman had to be made to take an interest in her daughter. Both of them could benefit from that.

Lori dug herself out of the sofa. She couldn't imagine what it was like, not having parents who loved and cared about you. Hers had been taken from her all too soon, but she had nothing but warm memories of both her mother and her father.

The lack of good parenting had been one of the things that had drawn her to Kurt. His charm had only been enough to bring her in at the beginning. But there was this lost little boy beneath it all, a lost boy who'd never experienced parental warmth. Who'd grown up without it. From what he had told her, his father had left when he was still very young and his mother had found her way into a bottle for solace. It was Carson who had raised him. Who had taken care of both Kurt and their mother from the time he was fifteen.

She supposed that explained a lot about Carson.

That kind of responsibility was hard on kid. Carson had worked hard at his education and after school, he took any job he could to help out. And somehow, he'd still found a way to be there for Kurt.

She knew Carson blamed himself for what had happened to Kurt. But the fact that Kurt was always drawn to the wild side, to speed, wasn't Carson's fault. He'd done the best he could to make a responsible person out of him. A man could only do so much.

But first, she mused, looking at the receiver still in her hand, they had to try. There was no way she was about to give up on Angela. It looked as if too many people had done that already.

She placed the receiver back in its slot, then made her way to the kitchen.

The refrigerator was as user unfriendly now as it had been this morning when she'd take out the last of the orange juice. She'd made a mental note to go shopping, but the day had gotten away from her and she'd forgotten all about going to the supermarket.

Not enough hours in the day, she thought, shaking her head. She let the door shut again. Oh well, it wouldn't hurt to skip a meal now and then.

She glanced down at her middle. It wasn't as if she was in any danger of wasting away. She'd done enough eating for two lately.

The sound of the doorbell caught her by surprise. She wasn't expecting anyone. Because of her erratic hours, her friends weren't in the habit of dropping by without warning.

The doorbell rang a second time before she got to

the front door. She looked through the peephole, but the image on the other side of the door wasn't clear. She told herself she needed to get one of those surveillance cameras for outside the door. The list of things she needed was mounting. First and foremost, she needed a fairy godmother.

"Who is it?" she asked.

Didn't she see that it was him? "Open the door, Lori," he said impatiently.

Carson?

She'd just left him in the parking lot. What was he doing here?

She opened the door before the silent question was completely formed in her brain. The man on her doorstep was holding a large brown bag against his chest and looked rather uncertain for Carson.

She smiled at him. "Hi."

"Hi."

Was it her imagination, or did he sound almost a little sheepish? Or was that awkward? She supposed, under the circumstances, that she felt a little awkward herself right now, given what had happened in the parking lot.

Carson cleared his throat. "I, um, haven't had any dinner yet."

She laughed, thinking of her refrigerator. Carson had been over a few times for dinner, but this wasn't going to be one of those evenings. "I'm afraid you're out of luck here unless you happen to like baking soda or wilted celery, or broccoli that looks as if it's about to mutate into another life-form."

He felt as if a Boy Scout jamboree had used his tongue to practice their knot-making.

"No. I mean, I picked up some." He hoisted the bag, using it as a visual aid. "Mexican food. Then I remembered that you liked Mexican food, too, so I got extra. I figured you hadn't eaten either." Why was she making this so hard for him? Eating should have been a simple matter.

She knew that he would probably tell her it was silly, but she was really touched by the gesture. "No, I haven't." He was still standing on her doorstep. All six foot two of him still looked miserably awkward. It wasn't like Carson. She gestured for him to come in. "That was very nice of you."

He snorted, pushing the compliment and her thanks away as if it was a bomb about to detonate right in front of him.

"Don't make a big deal out of this." Carson pushed the door closed behind him. "Can't have you neglecting to feed the baby."

She grinned, leading the way to the kitchen. Mexican food had been her main craving of choice. "At this rate, he or she'll probably be born wearing a sombrero and humming Mexican music."

Carson placed the bag down on the kitchen counter. He was surprised by her comment. "That's stereotyping."

"No disrespect intended." She carefully unpacked the foam boxes out of the bag. "Stereotypes are usually rooted in reality. Besides, I love Mexican music. And Mexican jewelry and don't even get me started about the food."

Though her pale coloring gave no indication to the casual observer, her mother had been part Mexican. The meals Lori remembered her mother preparing still made her mouth water every time she thought about them. Some of her best memories involved standing beside her mother in the kitchen, helping her make the dishes that were such a staple in their house when she was young.

Opening the cupboard, Lori stood on her toes in order to take down two dinner plates from the second shelf. Without thinking, Carson reached in and took them down for her. Surprised, Lori turned around, brushing her abdomen against him.

He stepped back as quickly as if he'd been brushed by a flaming torch instead of a pregnant woman. "You're shorter," he pointed out, mumbling his excuse for lending a hand.

She glanced down at her feet. She didn't usually walk around barefoot in front of him. "I'm not wearing my shoes."

He grasped at the topic with gratitude. Unlike most of the women in his acquaintance, Lori had worn high heels ever since he'd met her. Even through her pregnancy. "How you can wear those heels at a time like this—"

She shrugged. She was so used to wearing them she didn't even think about it.

"I can't remember a time when I didn't wear high heels. Besides," she confessed, "they make me feel pretty." Shoes had always been her weakness and she thought there was nothing more attractive than a nice pair of three- or four-inch heels.

He opened one of the containers. Splitting the enchiladas between them, he scooped out the sauce, spreading it evenly on the two plates. "You don't need shoes for that."

She set the two glasses she was holding on the table and looked at him, a smile playing across her lips. Would wonders never cease?

"Why, Carson, is that a compliment?"

"No," he retorted. Why did she have to make a big deal out of a conversation? "I mean…it's just an observation, that's all."

He used the excuse of getting napkins out of the pantry to turn away from her, afraid that he was going to trip over a tongue that had suddenly gotten too long and thick for him to manage properly.

What the hell was he doing here, anyway? He'd had every intention of going home after she'd left the center. But then his stomach began to growl, reminding him that he hadn't eaten for most of the day. Stopping at the Tex-Mex restaurant had reminded him of her. As if she had gotten very far out of his mind.

He wasn't in the mood to eat alone tonight. God only knew why. He usually preferred his own company to anyone else's. That way, there was no need to make idle conversation.

Except that with Lori, the conversation wasn't idle. It jumped around like an entity with a life of its own. Pretty much the way she did most of the time.

He shrugged carelessly, completely wrapped up in what he was doing. Or trying to look that way. "Nobody's looking at your feet anyway."

"I know." She patted her stomach. Was it her

imagination, or had it gotten bigger since this morning? She was beginning to feel like the incredible expanding woman. "They're all looking at my stomach." She paused, fisting one hand at what had once been her waist. "Why is it that when a woman's pregnant, people can't keep their eyes off her stomach?"

He looked at her. Her eyes always got to him. Her eyes and her smile. "That's not true."

She knew he was just saying that to be nice. "Well, it feels like it's true." She placed two sets of silverware out. "I feel like everyone's eyes are on my middle, waiting for something to happen."

He threw out the empty container for her and opened another. This one contained nachos with a cheese sauce. "Maybe you think they're expecting that because that's how you feel."

She moved the nachos to the middle of the table. "So now who's practicing psychoanalysis?"

He never lost a beat. "I'm a lawyer. Comes with the territory," he reminded her.

Pulling her chair out, she sat down. He straddled a chair opposite her. Like a cowboy about to go running off to a trail drive.

"So it does, Counselor." She studied him for a moment, thinking of the way he'd looked when she'd walked in on him at the center. Wondering if he'd think that she was prying if she asked. "Do you ever regret giving it up?"

He thought he would. When he'd gone for his degree, he'd been sure that was what he wanted to do with his life. But arguing in court, trying to get a man free on a technicality, never taking into account whether or not that man was actually innocent, was something that never felt quite right to him.

It wasn't until he'd turned his life in another direction that it finally felt as if he was doing the right thing.

"No," he said honestly, "oddly enough, I don't. Maybe because I don't have time to." He laughed shortly. "The one who regretted my giving it up was Jaclyn." The arguments had started in earnest then. And he got to see the darker side of the woman he'd fallen in love with. It was a rude awakening. "My taking over at the center didn't jibe with the vision of life she had in mind." He didn't hurt talking about her anymore. He didn't feel anything. It was as if that had all happened to someone else in another lifetime. "Guess she has it now."

Lori wasn't about to let him just throw out the comment and not follow it up. "Oh?"

He reached for a nacho. There was rabid interest on her face. "Didn't I tell you?"

He wasn't exactly the male equivalent of Chatty Cathy and they both knew it. "Carson, you never tell me anything without my jabbing you with a dose of Sodium Pentothal."

It was old news anyway, more than six months in the past. "She married some Beverly Hills plastic surgeon. Has a house in Bel Air, a housekeeper, everything she ever wanted."

Lori could feel that wall rising up again. The one he kept himself barricaded behind. Lori reached across the small table and placed her hand over his. "Except a good man."

He shrugged. Conscious of the warmth of her hand, he withdrew his. "I had him checked out. I still keep in touch with my old firm's P.I. Her new husband seems a decent enough guy."

"Why'd you have him checked out?" Unless, she thought, he still had feelings for his ex that he wasn't willing to admit to.

Carson thought that would have been self-evident. "If he was going to be living with my daughter, he damn well better not have any skeletons in his closet."

She should have realized that was it. She'd seen him with the kids at the center, gruff, but protective beneath all that. "You know, you're full of surprises, Carson O'Neill, you really are."

She was doing it again, making him feel like squirming. He nodded at her plate. "Your enchilada's getting cold. I know it's nothing like what you make, but in a pinch—"

He was apologizing again. "Don't knock it." She savored a bite. "It tastes *so* much better when I don't have to make it myself."

He'd sampled her cooking and this couldn't hold a candle to hers. "Funny, I was just thinking how much better it tasted when you made it."

The compliment pleased her. Whether he realized it or not, he was good for her. "Then I'll have to have you over for dinner again some night."

He frowned, lowering his eyes to his plate. "I wasn't fishing for an invitation."

She knew that. "Well, guess what? You caught one anyway."

"But—"

She wasn't about to let him wiggle out of it. He'd done a nice thing for her and she wanted to return the favor. End of discussion. "Shut up and pass the nachos, Carson."

There were times when he knew it was pointless to try to argue with her. He did as he was told.

Chapter Five

Restless, Lori tossed the magazine back on the square marble tabletop. Dr. Sheila Pollack, her OB-GYN, made a practice of keeping current with the reading material in the tastefully decorated waiting room, but since she'd already been here three times this month for herself, Lori'd read everything of interest to her. The rest of the magazines were devoted to how those with money to burn decorated their homes and that certainly didn't include her.

She glanced at her watch, wondering how much longer Angela's exam was going to take. The door leading to the four exam rooms remained closed no matter how many times she looked expectantly at it.

She'd been the one to bring Angela here today. Every time she'd asked the girl if she'd made an appointment with a doctor, Angela had put her off, procrastinating. After three days of verbal waltzing, Lori had called her own doctor. Lisa, Dr. Pollack's nurse, had been sympathetic and agreed to slip Angela in to see the doctor in between patients.

This state of limbo about Angela's condition was unacceptable.

"Why do you care?" Angela had demanded when she'd cornered her just as the girl had walked into the center this afternoon and told her that she'd made the arrangements for her to see a doctor.

Lori'd ushered her out of the building. They had to leave immediately.

"Because I do, that's all. You need to face this, one way or another." She'd pointed out her car. "Now let's go."

Braced for an argument, she didn't get one. Angela made no further protest about the pending exam. She also didn't talk very much on the trip to Dr. Pollack's office in Bedford.

Mercifully, because the traffic on the freeway was flowing, they reached the Bedford medical complex across the street from Blair Memorial in a little under twenty minutes.

The wait inside turned out to be longer. As Angela sat fidgeting beside her, it was almost forty-five minutes before there was a free exam room. Angela had wanted to leave twice and had actually gotten up once, but she allowed herself to be talked into remaining. Lori had a feeling the girl just wanted someone to force her to find out. Wanted someone to care enough to find out.

And now Angela was in exam room one, finding out if her life was going to be forever altered. Lori couldn't help feeling nervous for her.

Lori stared down at her nails. All Dr. Pollack had to do was give her a pelvic and she'd known immediately that she was pregnant. Why was it taking so long with Angela?

She knew she had absolutely no say in this matter one way or another, but if Angela was pregnant, she was going to try to talk the girl into having the baby and then considering her options after that. Maybe Angela's mother would finally find some maternal feelings and come through for her.

At the very least, Angela could give the baby up for adoption. Teaching the Lamaze classes had made her realize that there were so many people out there longing for a child of their own. If Angela had her baby and then gave it up for adoption, she'd be giving the gift of life to not only her child, but to the couple who would be adopting him or her.

The door leading back to the waiting room finally opened.

For one beat, Lori held her breath, mentally practicing her speech and crossing her fingers that Angela would be receptive.

There were tears on the girl's cheeks. She was pregnant. Lori was on her feet instantly. The next second, she was hugging the girl to her as the other three women in the waiting room looked on.

"Honey, it's okay. I'll be there for you," she promised.

But Angela drew away, shaking her head. "No."

Lori ignored the presence of the other women in the room. "I know you don't think so now, but—"

Angela was still shaking her head. "No, you don't

understand." And then she grabbed Lori's arms urgently. "I'm not pregnant. All this stuff at home, all this tension with my mom and my boyfriend, it's made me late, that's all. I'm not pregnant," she repeated. Her voice vibrated with overwhelming relief.

Lori blew out a breath, vicariously sharing the teenager's relief. Okay, she thought, no speech necessary. Catastrophe averted. She slipped an arm around the girl's slim shoulders.

"C'mon, let's go back to the center."

Suddenly too emotional to say another word, Angela just nodded. Lori opened the door and guided her out of the office.

She gave Angela some time to really absorb the situation and to calm down. She knew the girl must have been terrified as she waited for the pelvic exam to be over. Dr. Pollack had a wonderfully comforting bedside manner, but that still didn't take the edge off the fear Angela had gone in with. One look at her face when she'd followed the nurse into the inner office had said it all.

As she turned down the block to the teen center, Lori glanced at Angela. The girl had been incredibly quiet all the way back, not even attempting to change the radio station to find more contemporary music, the way she had on the way there.

Though the news was good, Lori couldn't help wondering if a part of Angela was somehow just a little disappointed just the same. This was a bittersweet situation that required delicate negotiation.

Lori knew all about emotions being all over the map. Hers had been doing that for a long while now.

"You dodged a bullet that time, Angela. There's a lesson to be learned here."

"Yeah, I'll say." Lori saw the girl's profile harden. "I thought Vinnie loved me. He said he'd always love me, no matter what. But once I told him I thought I was pregnant, the S.O.B. said he didn't want anything to do with me. He said if I was pregnant, it wasn't his. Like I'd ever slept with anyone else." Angela looked at her, her voice impassioned. "I'm not like that, Lori."

She reached for Angela's hand and gave it a quick squeeze. "I know that, honey. But there's a bigger lesson here than finding out the kind of guy Vinnie is. Sex isn't a game, Angela, it's a responsibility."

"Is that what you learned?"

She heard the defensiveness in the girl's voice. She didn't want Angela to think she was criticizing her or lecturing to her. "I was married."

Angela flushed. "Sorry, I didn't mean that." She bit one of her fingernails. "I kinda mouth-off when I get mad."

Lori smiled at her. "I noticed." And then she thought about her own life. "But, in a way, I suppose I'm a pretty good example of all the things that a woman has to think about before she does decide to get pregnant. You have to finish your education before you start a family so that you're better equipped to provide for your baby in case something happens. All sorts of things happen in life that you're not ready for. My husband died, my company went bankrupt and I had to scramble to make a living so that when this baby comes, I can provide for it. I've got a college degree and I'm a lot older than you are, Angela.''

Angela's head bobbed up and down vigorously. ''I'll say.''

Lori got out of the car and looked at the girl over the hood of her car. Nothing like a teenager to make you feel old, she thought.

''Hey, not *that* much older. But what I'm saying here is that you've got all the time in the world for this when you get older, Angela. Don't rush out of your teens. Don't rush to take on responsibilities that shouldn't be there for you until you've had time to be fifteen and eighteen and twenty. And carefree.''

Angela bit down on her lower lip, as if she was actually mulling over the advise instead of blocking it out. ''I guess that makes sense.''

And then she flashed a smile that warmed Lori's heart. ''Of course it makes sense.'' Lori opened the rear door to the center for her. ''Now don't you have a game to practice for?''

''Yeah,'' Angela beamed, looking very much like a fifteen-year-old who'd had the weight of the world lifted off her shoulders. ''I do.'' And then she surprised Lori by throwing her arms around her and hugging her. ''Thanks,'' she mumbled against her shoulder.

The next minute, Angela bolted and rushed into the building.

And that, Lori thought, was the way a fifteen-year-old was supposed to behave. Impulsive and happy.

''What was that all about?''

Startled, the door handle slipped out of her hand. She swung around to see Carson standing almost behind her. Where had he come from?

She took in a breath, then released it. Her stomach felt oddly jumbled, as if it was under attack. When *would* this baby stop tap dancing? It had been doing it for the past twenty-four hours or so. "Who let you out of your cage?"

He'd been worried. When he hadn't seen her for the past two hours, he'd assumed that she hadn't been feeling well and had decided to go home. It wasn't like her to leave without saying something. Calling her at home had gotten him nowhere. Calling the hospital had done the same.

He hadn't known what to think. Leaving Rhonda in charge, he'd gone out for a walk to try to channel this sudden directionless energy that was threatening to undo him. He'd just turned a corner when he'd seen Lori's car pull up. He'd lost no time in hurrying over.

"I wanted to clear my head," he told her.

She looked up at the sky. It was one of those hazy days that people associated with Southern California. "Too much smog out here for that today."

He knew what she was trying to do. "I've gotten used to it and don't change the subject. Where the hell have you been and what's up with Angela?"

She knew she should have told him before she left, but she also knew that he would have tried to talk her out of it, or flat-out told her she couldn't do this because there were rules to consider. All she could consider was Angela's welfare.

"I took her to see my gynecologist."

Carson's chiseled jaw dropped almost an inch. "Lori—"

She held up her hands before he could launch into a lecture. "I know, I know, I was meddling and I'm not supposed to, but damn it, Carson, the girl thought she was pregnant."

Dark brows gathered like storm clouds. "The girl also has a mother."

"So? Ma Barker was also a mother. She got her sons killed. And then there was Catherine de' Medici. She had scores of children. She also loved poisoning anyone she thought was her enemy—"

At times, her penchant for being a walking trivia trove got annoying. "I don't need a random history lesson, Lori. We're talking about parental rights here."

"No," she contradicted passionately. "We're talking about a young girl's life." She stuck her chin out pugnaciously. "You didn't talk to Angela's mother, Carson. I did. Or tried to. She sounded like she could care less about her daughter." She fisted her hands where her waist would have been under different circumstances, ready to fight him on this. "And if you're going to talk about rights, what about Angela's rights? What about her right to peace of mind?"

She could make a statue want to cover its ears. "Don't play lawyer with me, Lori. You won't win." His anger was calm, controlled. And maybe a little intimidating for all its quiet. "I wouldn't be here if I didn't care about the rights of these kids and what they're entitled to. I also know we wouldn't be able to survive a lawsuit. It would shut St. Augustine's down.''

In her opinion, there were far too many lawyers in the world, ready to go to battle and disrupt lives over petty issues. She was secretly glad that Carson had left those ranks.

''What lawsuit?'' she demanded heatedly. ''I just took her into my doctor so that she could find out if she was pregnant or not. She's not about to tell her mother I did that. She wants to put the whole thing behind her. Angela and her mother aren't exactly the *Gilmore Girls*.''

''All right, so what did you find out? Is she pregnant?''

Her anger melted into a smile. He liked watching the transformation and told himself he shouldn't. ''No, stress is throwing her timing off, that's all. She also got a little education in the fickleness of young studs.'' He raised his eyebrow, waiting for Lori to elaborate. ''She told her boyfriend she thought she was pregnant and he split. Said it wasn't his. His undying love died.'' She shook her head. The girl was looking for love in all the wrong places. ''Damn near broke her heart.''

That sounded far too sensitive for the girl he was acquainted with. ''She said that?''

''She didn't have to. Her eyes did.''

''You read eyes now?''

She looked up into his. Still as unfathomable as always, she thought. Most of the time, the man was a walking mystery to her. But that didn't mean she wasn't willing to try to change that. "I read anything that'll give me a clue."

"Lori, you're going to turn my hair gray."

She cocked her head, trying to picture him with streaks of gray woven through his black hair. "Gray looks good on some men. Makes them distinguished."

He laughed shortly, shaking his head. "You've got an answer for everything, don't you?"

"Pretty much."

"You should have been the lawyer." The other side would have been waving a white flag in no time, Carson thought.

She grinned. "If I had been, I would have given you a run for your money."

His eyes slid over her abdomen. "Right now, I don't want to see you running anywhere. Matter of fact, I'd rather not see you, period."

"You know you don't mean that." She patted his face. "I light up your day."

The ironic thing was, he thought as opened the door for her and they walked back into the building, she was right. Not that he was ever going to tell her. If she knew, there'd be no living with her.

There was hardly any living with her now.

Despite the fact that the baby insisted on being restless, Lori spent the rest of the day at the center. She'd seen all the kids off, had talked to Angela again before the girl went home and had told Rhonda that she would lock up. There were no Lamaze classes tonight and she didn't relish the idea of going home just yet.

She wondered if Carson was in the mood to catch a quick bite. Making her way to his office, she found him the way she had last week. Frowning over something on the computer.

Probably the budget again. He hadn't said a word about her idea since she'd framed it for him. It was time to prod him. "So, have you given my suggestion any thought?"

Carson blinked as he looked away from the screen. No matter how long he stared, the number just wouldn't change. "What suggestion?"

Was he playing games, or had he really forgotten? "About the fund-raiser."

"No." He'd been hoping the impossible, that she would drop the matter.

The word had a final ring to it. She might have known. With Carson, everything was an uphill fight. "Why?"

"Because it was a dumb suggestion when you made it, and it's still a dumb suggestion now." He saw exasperation flit over her face and knew he was in for it. Trying to cut her off wasn't going to work, but he tried anyway. "Fund-raisers are for national causes, national charities. Medical research."

"Not everyone wants to toss their money into a large pile." He was an intelligent man, why didn't he know that? "There are a lot of people who feel better backing the little guy."

His mouth twisted into a cynical expression. "Well, they certainly don't come any littler than St. Augustine's."

Was he being sarcastic, or just downplaying the

center's influence on the neighborhood teens? She took offense for the center. And for him.

"Oh, I don't know. It's had positive effects on people's lives over the years. Look at how you turned out."

She struck a nerve. "Right. I don't think *People* magazine's going to be breaking down my door anytime soon, asking for an interview."

She wasn't about to let him throw stones, even at himself. *Especially* not at himself. "You were a kid who came from these mean streets and you became a successful lawyer."

That was only half the story. His ex had jeered the rest at him when she'd announced that she was going to get a divorce. "Who gave up working at a lucrative law firm to come back here and periodically bash his head against a wall."

That wasn't all there was to the story. "Because he was compassionate," Lori pointed out.

How could he argue with her when she was trying to defend him? He smiled despite himself. "Do you always have to have the last word?"

Her eyes danced as she looked up at him. "Only when I'm right."

"And just who decides that?"

"Me," Lori replied simply, knowing she was baiting him. "And God."

He sighed, shaking his head. Maybe he should call it a night after all. He was bone tired. It had been a long day. Carson pressed buttons on the keyboard, closing the computer down. "So now you talk to God."

"Every night."

"And does He talk back, or do you intimidate him, too?"

She honed in on what she took to be a slip. "Do I intimidate you?"

Carson gave her a look that was meant to put her in her place. "No, but you try."

"Do not," she countered glibly. "I just like to champion a cause, that's all." She frowned, wishing he'd listen to reason. She just *knew* the fund-raiser would erase that furrow between his eyebrows. At least temporarily. "And I hate seeing you being so stubborn when you're wrong."

He wondered what it felt like, to always feel you were right, to always be on the side of the angels. "Maybe I'm not."

"But maybe you are," she insisted. "Don't you think you owe it to yourself—and the center—to find out?"

Didn't she understand how presumptuous all this sounded? And how humiliating it could be? "What if we gave a fund-raiser and nobody came?"

Her parents had instilled the ability within her to always see the bright side of any situation. "Then the kids at the center would have a lot of good food to eat for a week." But that wasn't going to happen. She firmly believed that. "What if we didn't give a fund-raiser and people were willing to come?"

The woman just wouldn't stop, would she? "Lori, you're talking nonsense."

She took offense at the cavalier way he dismissed the idea. "I never thought you'd be afraid."

She knew just how to press his buttons, even when he thought he'd put a lock on them. "I'm not afraid, I just don't want to look like a fool."

Didn't he get it yet? "Caring about something doesn't make you a fool."

What did it take to pull the shades from her eyes? And why did a woman who had so much go wrong for her seem determined to continue looking at life through rose-colored glasses?

"But thinking that I can get other people to care about what I care about just on my say-so does. Don't you understand that? Now drop this, Lori, before you make me lose my temper."

She frowned at him. *Stubborn idiot.* "Is that supposed to make me shake in my shoes?"

He could feel his temper beginning to fray. "It's supposed to make you stop babbling, although I'm beginning to think only duct tape will accomplish that."

Yelling at him had never been the way to win. She tried again. "Let me talk to my friends," she pleaded. "You know I'm right."

Enough was enough. Standing up, he towered over her. "What I know is that if you don't stop nagging, I'm going to have to fire you."

Her eyes narrowed. "You wouldn't dare. You need me."

He'd gone too far to make a U-turn now. "Try me."

"You'd really fire me?"

"If you don't stop, yes." Why wouldn't she just back off? Something had to make her.

Anger flared in her eyes. "All right, then, maybe I'll just quit."

Damn it, this had gone too far. Why didn't she ever cry "uncle"? "You can't apply for unemployment if you quit."

"Oh, so now you're worried about me?"

He flipped the computer back on. He was staying. Adrenaline had just given him his second wind. "Damn it, Lori, I'm always worried about you. Now go home and let me try to squeeze blood out of a stone."

"The only stone I see is the rock between your ears. Now if you—"

She stopped so abruptly, he looked up. She was wincing and her face was pale. "What's the matter?"

Lori had trouble drawing the air back into her lungs. It had all but whooshed out of her when the tap dance the baby was doing had turned into a Charleston. At double-speed.

Followed by an incredible surge of unadulterated pain.

Lori looked down at the floor and then at him with stunned amazement vibrating through her. This was too early. She wasn't supposed to be early.

There was no arguing with the facts. "I think my water just broke."

It was happening.

Chapter Six

She had to be kidding, Carson thought. Her water hadn't broken. She wasn't due yet. These kinds of things happened dramatically only in sitcoms and movies.

"Look, if this is some kind of ploy to try to get me to see things your way—"

But the look on her face told him that he had better start taking this seriously.

Lori splayed her hand over his desk, her fingers spreading out as far as they could reach. Pain was vibrating through every part of her body. This hurt like the devil.

"Trust me, I'm not that good." She measured out every word, as if there wasn't enough air to make it to the end of her sentence if she wasn't careful. "If you want visual proof—"

Carson was on his feet instantly. He rounded the desk and hurried over to her side. Damn it, why now?

Why not when she was with some female friends who had a clue what to do?

He peered at her face, hoping against hope that it was a false alarm. "You're sure?"

She stared straight ahead, afraid to even move her eyes. Afraid that if she did, the pain would suddenly accelerate. "Uh-huh."

His brain refused to absorb the information. Or maybe he was hoping that if he denied it enough, it would cease to be true. "You're in labor."

"Oh, yeah."

She said it with such conviction, all hope to the contrary died. Did he touch her? Offer support? Keep clear in case she needed space? He felt like an alien in a foreign land. "What do you want me to do?"

The pain was taking a step backward. It was becoming manageable. She slanted her eyes toward him. "Knocking me out sounds pretty good about now."

If she could quip, then maybe the situation wasn't as dire as he thought. But there was one thing he knew for sure. "I've got to get you to the hospital."

Lori tested the waters slowly and nodded her head just a fraction of an inch. The pain was withdrawing, taking its sharp, pointy instruments with it. Thank God.

"Second best," she allowed, although oblivion still held its allure. This was just the beginning and part of her didn't feel as if she was going to be up to it. No choice, she thought.

Very slowly, she released her grip on the desk and covered her belly protectively with her hand.

Carson never took his eyes off her. Should he put

her in his chair and push her out to the car? Carry her? He'd never felt so unsure about what to do in his life. "Can you walk?"

A half a smile curved her mouth. Amid her fear that the pain would return, twice as strong, twice as big, at any moment was a sweetness that was flittering over her soul. She couldn't recall ever hearing Carson sound this gentle, this concerned.

"My legs still work, Carson. It's my middle that's under attack."

If she wasn't asking him to carry her, he wasn't going to volunteer. Dignity was an important factor to every human being. He left her with hers. "Okay, then let's go."

"Right."

She wanted to walk out on her own power. She'd had a thing about hanging tough, especially since Kurt had died. But the weakness that was assaulting her knees drove nails of fear through her. She looked at Carson, not saying a word.

She didn't have to. He slipped his arm around her shoulders, silently giving her the support she needed.

Lori blessed him for it.

Once outside, he guided her over to his car. She looked back at hers, parked three spaces over against the building. "What about my car?"

This was no time to launch into a debate over which car to use. He'd driven the sedan today and his was the roomier vehicle. He had a feeling that she was going to need all the space she could get right now.

"I'll have someone drive me back for it and I'"

drop it off at your house.'' One arm around her, he
took out his key and unlocked the passenger side.
''Your car's the least of your problems right now.''
Very slowly he lowered her onto the seat and then
helped her swing her legs inside. He didn't bother
masking his concern when he looked at her. ''You
sure you don't want me to call 9-1-1?''

If anyone had ever asked her, she would have said
that Carson was incapable of being this gentle. Who
would have thought?

She did what she could to assuage his concern.
''No 9-1-1. I'm just in labor, Carson, not in the early
stages of delivery.''

He had his doubts. Lori had this superwoman attitude about her that got in her way more than once.
Especially now. He didn't want to take any unnecessary chances. ''You sure?''

He kept asking her that. She could feel the edges
of her temper peeling away and knew she was being
unreasonable. With effort, she curbed her tongue.
''As sure as I can be.'' She looked at him as he got
in behind the wheel, turning only her head, afraid a
new onslaught of pain might start at any sudden
movement. ''Hey, I'm new at this kind of thing,
Carson. I'm playing it by ear.''

He turned on the ignition. ''It's not your ear I'm
concerned about.''

Lori's eyes fluttered shut, as if that could somehow
seal the pain away from her. ''Just drive,'' she
breathed.

Something was happening. She wasn't sure if it
was a contraction, but it felt like it might be one. If

not, some invisible force was going at her with a giant, jagged can opener in one hand, a sledgehammer in the other. How could women have more than one baby after going through this?

He started to put the car into drive, then saw that she still hadn't buckled up. "Get your seat belt on," he ordered.

Lori grabbed the strap, trying to pull it around herself but it wouldn't give. "How about if I just brace my feet against the floor and you drive as fast as you can?"

Now she was scaring him. Maybe he should just call the paramedics. "That bad?"

She shifted her eyes toward him and tried to smile, knowing he needed to see the effort more than she needed to make it. "It's not good." Her throat felt dry as she swallowed. "Just get me to Blair, please, Carson."

It was all she needed to say. He reached over and pulled the seat belt up and over her bulk, then sank the tongue into the groove, snapping it in place.

"I'll get you there as fast as I can," he promised.

Couldn't be fast enough for her, she thought. "Sounds good to me."

Gunning the engine, Carson peeled out of the small parking lot behind the center. He made his way onto the street, snaking in front of a deep purple Camaro. The latter's driver leaned down on his horn in protest over the sudden maneuver. Carson never looked back.

Amber lights blinked, on their way to becoming red as Carson sped through one light after the other, his goal the southbound freeway. Somehow, he managed to make it through each light before it turned red.

"If you're trying to scare me into delivering the baby in the car, you just might be successful."

He didn't even spare her a look, his eyes intent on the road.

"That's exactly what I'm trying to prevent." The last thing in the world he wanted was for her to have the baby with only him in attendance. The very idea scared the hell out of him. All he could think of was that women still died in childbirth.

He made it to the on-ramp of the 405. Like a racer at the Indianapolis 500, Carson wove his car in and out of the various lanes of traffic until he finally crossed over firmly painted double yellow lines and merged into the carpool lane a full fifty feet before it was legally allowed.

Lori was afraid to hold her breath, afraid that if she did, if would somehow terminate her labor and throw her headfirst into the delivery. But her pulse was definitely racing as she watched Carson's progress.

"You could get a ticket for that." The words came out breathlessly.

"A cop would be nice around now." He glanced in his rearview mirror. No such luck. "He'd get us to the hospital faster."

She managed to find the control on the armrest and pressed until the window rolled down. She was perspiring so much she was afraid she was going to dissolve in a puddle soon. "So this racing madly and breaking laws is actually a plan."

"I've always got one."

It sounded good, but it was a lie. Carson liked to think that most if not all of his life was proceeding according to schedule if not some kind of outright plan. But lately, he had to admit he'd been flying by the seat of his pants. It had begun with his divorce, which had hit him with the force of a small-time bomb. His brother's death the following year had devastated him. And now this thing that hummed between Lori and him confounded him so totally he had trouble remembering what day it was. If there was still some kind of a plan to his life, other than running the center, it had somehow gotten lost in the shuffle. The only plan life seemed to have for him was chaos.

He glanced at Lori as he pressed down on the gas pedal. The speedometer needle was flirting with numbers that went far above the ones posted on the speed limit signs. He saw that Lori had one hand braced on the dashboard. Her knuckles were white. Was that from the pain?

What else would it be, idiot? he mocked himself. "How are you doing?"

She was trying to breathe as regularly as possible. All she really wanted to do was scream in frustration. "I've been better."

He took the connection to the 55 southbound, telling himself that it wouldn't be that much longer. "Damn it, Lori, why didn't you go home the way I've been telling you to?"

Here it came again, that pain that took her entire body prisoner, squeezing every part of her. She struggled to stay grounded. "If I had, I'd be going through this alone right now."

That wasn't his point. He zipped around a car that was going too slow for him, mentally cursing at the driver. "You'd also be closer to the hospital and maybe if you weren't so hell-bent on doing everything as if you weren't pregnant, you wouldn't have gone into labor in the first place."

That was unrealistic and they both knew it. "I've been circling my due date for days now. I would have had to have gone into labor eventually." She looked at his stony profile. Was he angry at her? No, that wasn't it. She realized he was worried about her, but she wished he could show it with soft words instead of snapping at her. "Just not around you." She clenched her hands in her lap as another wave began to roll over her. She pushed the question out before she couldn't form it. "Would you have preferred it that way?"

"Yes," he bit off.

Well, Carson was nothing if not honest, she thought. He wasn't given to charming lies, the way Kurt had been. She'd seen that as one of Kurt's shortcomings. Still, right now she would have liked to be lied to. She couldn't even say why. Or why she suddenly felt like crying.

"I see. Well, when we pull up at the hospital, you can just push me out the door," she retorted. "I'll roll right in. You don't even have to come to a full stop."

He hadn't meant to hurt her feelings. The sting of guilt had his anger flaring higher. "Damn it, Lori, I just mean I'm not any good at this."

That made two of them. Lori struggled to get a grip on her fear. "Neither am I."

"But you taught Lamaze classes at the hospital," he pointed out. "You had all that background training. You know what's coming." As far as he was concerned, the whole process was as mysterious as plucking a rabbit out of a magician's hat.

As if any of her training helped, she thought in disgust. "Knowing what's coming and being caught right in the middle of it are two entirely different things." She tried to think of something a man could relate to. "It's the difference between watching a war movie and being smack in the middle of a real battle."

"Point taken." The off-ramp was right ahead. He'd made a twenty minute trip in ten. "We're almost there. Won't be long now."

Oh God, here came another one of those things. Even harder than before. It wasn't supposed to be happening this way. She wasn't ready yet. Maybe in another year. "Easy for you to say," she panted.

He didn't like the sound of that. Why was she making those noises? He looked at her. "Lori?"

She shook her head, not answering. Instead, her eyes were fixed on some nebulous point beyond the windshield and she was taking short pants the way she'd shown other women how to do countless times in the class.

Except that this time, it was for real.

She began to feel light-headed.

"Lori, what's going on?" he wanted to know.

"Why are you breathing like that?" Was she going to pass out on him?

She felt as if all the air had been let out of her. It was over, the strange urge to expel all of her organs at once had passed. For now.

Lori blew out a long, cleansing breath then looked at him. Why did he insist on annoying her with all these questions? "Weren't you at your daughter's birth?"

He shook his head. It was one of the main regrets of his life. "I was in the middle of a high profile trial." His mouth twisted grimly. "Jaclyn didn't want me there. She wanted the prestige of having me win."

Even in her present condition, she knew enough to try to navigate past the rapids and toward clearer waters. "Did you?"

"Yeah."

Her heart went out to him. "Then I guess she got what she wanted."

A sigh of resignation escaped his lips. "She always did."

Maybe it was dumb, but she'd never really played it safe when feelings were concerned. And she had a very tender spot in her heart for Carson. Jaclyn was cold for having treated him this way, like an object, a means to an end. He deserved better than that. He deserved someone who loved him for the man he was, not the man someone wanted him to be.

"But you didn't."

That was the mother of all understatements. "I missed Sandy's birth." He'd looked forward to that, counting the days. Jaclyn had tricked him. "I didn't even know she was in labor until after the fact. Jaclyn had gone in and had labor induced to get the whole thing over with.'' Those had been his ex-wife's words. She'd regarded the miracle of their daughter's birth as something odious to get out of the way.

Lori clutched the overhead strap, bracing herself for the next tidal wave of pain. "How did you ever get so caught up with such a calculating woman?''

He shrugged. Because he'd been lonely. Because Jaclyn had been a stunning woman and knew how to ply her trade. She'd seen him as her ticket to the right circles. All she had to do was get him there. But he'd been blind to all of that. All he'd seen was someone whom said she'd loved him, someone who he thought he loved.

"Seemed like a good idea at the time. Besides, Jaclyn wasn't calculating then. At least,'' he allowed, "not that I noticed.'' He supposed that had been his fault. "I was too busy proving myself at the firm.'' It all seemed like it had happened a million years ago.

They were off the freeway. There were only five more long blocks to the hospital.

"Almost there,'' he told her again, hoping that would put her at ease. Or as at ease as she possibly could be at a time like this.

"I'm holding you to that,'' she murmured, beginning to slip back into the web of pain with its steel threads. She shut her eyes tight.

And then she felt a sudden, abrupt jerk.

Lori opened her eyes and saw the line of cars before them. Just like that, traffic had come to almost a dead stop. It looked as if they were in the middle of a parking lot.

This couldn't be happening. She tried to sit up straight and succeeded only marginally. Her body felt as if it was rebelling against her. "What's going on?"

Carson swallowed a curse as he made a calculated guess. "Must be an accident up ahead. Maybe it'll clear up soon." Even as he said it, he didn't believe it. He looked at her. "Can you hang in there?"

She pressed her lips together and nodded, but Carson had serious doubts.

His view was obstructed by the tan SUV in front of him. Frustrated, Carson opened the door on the driver's side.

Lori looked at him. Was he leaving? "What are you doing?"

"Seeing how far this jam extends."

He got out and took hold of the roof, and then climbed up on the doorsill. The extra inches of visibility only showed him more traffic. A whole sea of traffic. It looked as if nothing was moving well past the hospital turn-off. In the distance, he thought he detected red and yellow lights, but that didn't do them any good here.

He got down again and looked into his vehicle.

"Well?" she asked.

He knew she wasn't going to like what he had to tell her. "Doesn't look like it's going to clear up anytime soon."

"Swell." Heat traveled up and down the sides of her body and the pointy instruments of pain were back, jabbing her in all the inappropriate places. She couldn't remain like this indefinitely. "So how do you feel about my delivering in your car?"

There was nowhere to pull off, nowhere to go in order to give her even the smallest measure of privacy. The road was straight and completely exposed all the way past Hospital Road.

There was only one thing to do. Straightening, Carson closed the door on his side.

Panic came crashing down, fueled by hormones that had gone completely awry. What was Carson doing? Where was he going?

She tried to crane her neck as he disappeared from view. The next thing she knew, he was opening the door on her side of the car. She looked at him in confusion. "What's going on?"

"We're going to have to walk there," he told her. He began to take her arm to help her out of her seat.

She pulled it back. "Maybe you, but not me." She was through trying to act tough. "I can't be John Wayne any longer."

Carson laughed dryly. "John Wayne wouldn't have been in this position," he assured her.

He tried to reassess the situation. They couldn't just stay here, waiting for the traffic to clear and he wasn't about to have her deliver her baby in the back of his car. It wasn't sanitary. Besides, all sorts of things could go wrong, not to mention that he didn't want her to have to deal with the embarrassment of having people possibly looking in and seeing her go through the ordeal.

He made up his mind. There was only one thing to do. "You don't have to walk."

"Flying is not an option." She was trying very, very hard to keep her growing panic at bay. Her hormones felt as if someone had loaded them into a slingshot and fired. Right now they were ricocheting all over the place.

"No flying," he assured her. Taking her by the arm, he eased her out. The next thing she knew, she was in Carson's arms.

Was he crazy? "Carson, you can't walk to the hospital carrying me like this."

He had already begun to walk. She was lighter than he'd expected, even with the extra weight. "Why not?"

"Because I'm too heavy." If she'd had the strength, she would have jumped down, but that was really not possible.

Carson smiled at her. "Been meaning to say something to you about that. You'd better cut out those extra starches."

She looked back at his vehicle. Had he even locked it? "What about your car?"

He was aware of the dirty looks that his abandoning the car had garnered. But once Lori was out of the vehicle, the horn blasts from the cars directly behind him had ceased. Everyone familiar with the area knew how close they were to Blair Memorial and the woman in his arms was very obviously pregnant. Adding two and two together wasn't difficult.

"It's not going anywhere."

She threaded her arms around his neck, knowing she needed to put up more of a protest. But it was hard when she was having trouble catching her breath. "I can't let you do this."

If he'd called 9-1-1, she'd be in better hands than his right now. He should have gone with his first instincts. All he could do now was get her there as fast as possible. "Don't see as how you have much say in the matter. Now stop talking, the hot air is making you heavier."

She looked at the road ahead of them. Tree-lined, it still made her think of San Francisco. "Carson, it's uphill all the way."

"Then you'll owe me. I'll remind you of this every time you start getting argumentative." He forced a smile to his lips as he looked down at her. "Guess we'll be talking about this a lot." He felt Lori stiffen against him. "Bad?"

"Not good," she murmured. God help her, it wasn't fair to him but she felt safe in his arms. Unable to do anything else, she buried her face against his shoulder. "Thank you, Carson."

Her warm breath penetrated through his shirt, spreading small waves of something he wasn't about to explore through his chest. "Don't see how I have much say in the matter, either."

That was so like him. "Just accept gratitude once in a while."

He shifted her weight slightly in his arms as he crossed the street and began up the next block. "I'll see what I can do."

Chapter Seven

Carson's stride lengthened as he came down the slight incline that led from the sidewalk to the rear entrance of Blair Memorial's Emergency Room. He knew he was jostling Lori with each step he took, but it couldn't be helped.

Her breathing was becoming labored. He could tell by the way she stiffened that she was struggling against another contraction. "Hang in there," he told her. "We're almost there."

She merely nodded in response, pressing her lips together.

"I've got a pregnant woman in labor here," he announced loudly the instant the ER electronic doors sprang open for him.

Within moments an orderly came rushing up, pushing a gurney before him. A nurse followed in the man's wake. Another nurse was on her heels. Questions were being fired at him from all directions.

"Are you the father?"

"Is she hurt?"

"How far along are her contractions?"

"Is her doctor on staff here? Has he been called yet?"

Carson tried to make sense of all the words coming at him. "No. No. I don't know. I think so. No." If there were any other questions in need of answers, he couldn't untangle them from the rest. He looked to Lori for clarification.

There was pain written across her face, but she was alert. For someone in the throes of labor, she still looked pretty damn good, he thought. But then, she'd always looked pretty damn good to him.

Lori wet her lips. In contrast to the rest of her, they were horribly dry. She wasn't even sure she could push the words out between them.

"My doctor's Dr. Sheila Pollack," she told the intern who came up to join the circle of people gathering around her. "There was no time to call her."

A low-level din rose in her ears, closing in around her senses.

Carson was moving back.

He was withdrawing.

Panicked, Lori raised herself up on her elbows just enough to grab hold of his forearm. Her fingers gripped it as tightly as she could manage.

"No." Dark eyes looked at her questioningly. "Stay," she entreated.

Very gently, he tried to disengage himself. For a little thing, Lori had one hell of a grip.

"Lori, they'll take care of you."

Not like he would, she thought frantically. She wanted him with her. Suddenly, she didn't feel like a superwoman—more like vulnerable and afraid. She needed his familiar face in her corner, because it would give her something to focus on.

"No, I want you." She looked at the fresh faced intern for support. "He's my coach," she told the bespectacled man.

Stunned, Carson stared at her. This was certainly news to him. She'd never even approached him with the slightest hint that she wanted him with her when she went into labor. There were certainly other places he wanted to be, up to and including the hull of the *Titanic*. "I'm your *what?*"

"Coach." She licked her lips, her tongue almost sticking to them. "Please?"

"Page Dr. Pollack," the intern instructed the taller of the two nurses. "Tell her one of her patients is about to deliver." He raised a brow as he looked at Lori. "I'm sorry, I didn't get your name."

It was Carson who snapped the answer out. "Lori O'Neill." She'd slid her fingers down to his wrist and had clamped a death grip around it. "Lori, you can't be serious. Where's your real coach?"

A contraction started. There wasn't much time for her to answer. She twisted and arched on the gurney. Why did it have to hurt like this? She knew that there were women who had gone through almost a painless delivery, why couldn't she be like one of them?

"I...don't...have...one."

She never ceased to amaze him. The woman taught

Lamaze classes, for heaven's sake. How could she not have a coach of her own?

The old saying about the shoemaker's children going barefoot struck a hard chord.

The ER head nurse shouldered Carson to the side. "If you're going to coach her," the heavyset woman advised, "you'd better come this way." She looked as if she would brook no nonsense, but her deep brown eyes were kind. "Maternity ward's on the fifth floor and we need to get her up there right away." She nodded toward the orderly. "You know the drill, Jorge."

A row of brilliant white teeth flashed as the short, powerful man took over the gurney and began pushing it out of the ER toward the service elevators.

All he had to do was stop walking. Pull his hand out of her grasp and stop walking, Carson thought. That was all. God knew he certainly didn't want to be part of something so intimate as the birth of Lori's baby.

He wasn't the baby's father and he and Lori were only...

They were close. He and Lori were close. And she needed him.

The argument was over before it was ever begun.

Easing his wrist out of her grasp, Carson took her hand in his and hurried along beside the gurney as the orderly guided it to the back elevators.

He wasn't cut out for this kind of thing. He didn't know how much more he could take.

They had placed Lori in one of the small birthing

rooms. It was cheerfully decorated in an effort to evoke a soothing atmosphere for the miracle that was wrestling its way into the world. But there was nothing cheerful about what Lori was going through.

He was standing beside Lori who was writhing in pain on the bed. The battle had been going on for over six hours with no end in sight.

Carson had never felt so damn useless in his whole life.

Exasperated, he looked at the maternal-looking woman who had just finished checking on Lori. "Can't you do something about this?" he demanded. "Look at her, she's in pain."

"Yes, sir, I know." The nurse's voice was calm, as peaceful as he felt agitated. "It's all part of the process."

That was no answer. "Well, part of the process is sadistic," he snapped.

Carson's voice peeled away the haze forming around her brain. Taking his hand, Lori offered the nurse an apologetic smile. "You'll have to…forgive him…. He…means well, but…his…social graces… are…the first…to go…under…fire."

The white-haired woman merely laughed, her ample bosom heaving. "Don't worry about me, honey. I've seen and heard them all. After fifteen years in maternity, I've got a hide like a rhino." She smiled at Carson as she exited the room. "Your wife'll be fine."

"She's not my wife," he protested, but the nurse had already left the room, on her way to the next station on the floor.

He said that with so much feeling, Lori thought. She felt guilty about forcing him to stay. "I'm sorry…for…putting you through…this." She tried to hurry her words out, afraid that any moment, another contraction would cut them short. The effort was draining. "You can…go…if you…want to."

Oh, he wanted to all right. Very much. But now that he was here, he couldn't just leave her. To walk out on her now when she was like this seemed almost inhuman, not to mention damn cowardly. Like it or not, she needed him and he was here for the duration.

He shrugged, looking down at her. "I can stick it out if you can. You've got the tougher assignment."

She tried to smile. "Tell me…about it." And then her eyes widened like exploding cornflowers and she squeezed his fingers hard.

"Another one?" It wasn't really a question. The way she was crushing his fingers told him all he needed to know. Carson wondered if he would ever fully regain the use of his right hand once this was over.

Unable to answer, Lori nodded. Pressing her lips together, she struggled to hold back the scream she felt gurgling in her throat.

Damn it, why couldn't he do something to help her? he thought angrily. Why couldn't *someone* do something? "The nurse said it wouldn't be long now," he repeated. The promise didn't comfort either one of them.

"All…depends…on your…perspective." Right now, it was feeling pretty much like an eternity to her.

He looked at the pink pitcher on the side table. Water was condensing along its sides like falling tear-drops. "Want some more ice chips?" He was already reaching for the pitcher, needing to do something besides look at her helplessly.

But Lori moved her head from side to side. Ice chips wouldn't help. Her mouth was dry the second the chips melted.

"Only…if they have…knock-out drops…in…them."

It was going to be over with soon. Soon, she promised herself. Lori tried to focus on a point in time in the future when this was behind her, but the pain kept anchoring her to the moment. There were only small respites now, far shorter than the waves of pain that came in their wake.

How much more could she take? she thought in desperation.

Taking out his handkerchief, Carson gently mopped her brow before the perspiration could fall into her eyes. Suddenly, every bone in her body looked like it was stiffening.

Lori bit back another scream. "Get…the…doctor!" she ordered, her voice gravelly.

He clutched her hand, giving her something to hold onto to. She cut off his circulation. "Why? What's wrong?"

Wrong? What did he think was wrong? She was exploding, that was what was wrong. "The baby's… coming."

He hesitated. She'd said this before. "It's been coming for the last six hours." Six years was more like it to him.

Why was he arguing with her? "Now... It's... coming...NOW," she insisted.

He'd already called the nurse into the room three other times. Each time Lori had been certain that the delivery was imminent, but she wasn't dilated far enough.

One look at Lori's face and any thoughts of trying to reason with her fled. Carson went to the door again.

He looked up and down the hallway. The nurse was just coming out of the room next to Lori's.

"I think she's ready this time."

The nurse was patience itself. There wasn't even a glimmer of skepticism on her face. "Then let's go see, shall we?"

Preceding him into the room, the nurse went straight to the foot of Lori's bed and positioned herself on the stool placed there. Carson looked away as she pulled back the sheet and examined Lori.

With a smile, the woman rose from the stool and dropped the sheet back into place. "Looks like this time, you're going to have yourselves a baby."

Carson stared at her in disbelief. He'd begun to feel that the baby was never going to come. "You mean she's really having it now?"

The nurse nodded. "That's what I mean." She looked at Lori. "You're completely effaced. Ten centimeters. I'll go get Dr. Pollack."

Lori dug her heels into the bed for traction. "Hurry," she pleaded.

The woman was already gone.

Alone with Lori, Carson sank his hands into his

pockets. He glanced toward the closed door. "I should go."

She looked at him, not comprehending the words. "What?"

How could a single word make him feel so guilty? It wasn't his place to be here. "This is too personal, Lori. You don't want me here."

Her head was spinning. "Yes." She pushed the word out between clenched teeth. One of the monitors moved as she raised her hips from the bed. There was no hiding place from this. "I…do."

Forming an arch, her whole body looked like a sine curve on a graph.

She put her hand out, her fingers fanning the air frantically, unable to reach him. He knew that all he had to do was just take a step away, then another and another until he reached the other side of the door.

He moved back to the bed. Back to Lori and what had somehow become his responsibility.

Taking her hand, he stroked her hair. "It's going to be all right."

She hung onto the assurance as if it was a lifeline pulling her out of the swirling whirlpool. Consumed by another contraction, harder than all the rest. "Promise?"

"Promise."

The look in her eyes told Carson she was grateful for the comfort. And for his remaining in the room with her.

A tall, slender blonde wearing green scrubs entered the room. "I hear we're having a baby in the next few minutes." Dr. Sheila Pollack gave off a calming, confident aura the moment she walked into the room. She looked at Carson. "Hello, I'm Dr. Sheila Pollack." Her smile was quick, confident. "But you've probably figured that part out by now."

"Carson O'Neill. I'm her brother-in-law," he felt compelled to add.

"Nice of you to be here, Carson." Sheila took Lori's other hand in hers and gave it a comforting squeeze. "Ready to bring this baby in?"

"More...than...ready."

"Then let the games begin." Sheila flashed her a smile and positioned herself at the foot of the bed. She moved the sheet aside. One quick look was all that was needed. "Oh yes, I'd say that you were more than ready. It's a lovely evening for a baby to be born."

"I...can...push?" It was all she'd wanted to do for the past half hour.

Sheila nodded. "Absolutely. On my count." She raised her eyes to Carson, her smile encouraging. "I want you behind her, Carson, supporting her shoulders. Raise her off the bed," she instructed. When he complied, she nodded. "That's it. All right, Lori, this is it. On three. One—two—three. Push!"

Lori squeezed her eyes shut, squeezed with the rest of her body as well. She held her breath as she pushed as hard as she was physically able.

She was beginning to feel light-headed when she heard Sheila order, "All right, stop."

She fell back, exhausted, against Carson's hands. They felt strong, capable and all she wanted to do was somehow shrink down into nothingness and hide within them. But then she stiffened as another contraction seized her in its jaws.

Sheila looked at the monitor, seeing the contraction before it arrived. "Okay, Lori, again. One—two—three, push!"

Lori had no choice in the matter. It was as if the baby, eager to finally come into the world, pushed for her. Holding her breath, she bore down so hard, bursts of light began to dance through her head and behind her shut eyelids.

Propping her up, Carson brought his face in close to hers from behind. "Can't you do a C-section?" he prodded the doctor. This didn't seem right, having someone suffer like this.

"She doesn't need a C-section," Sheila assured him. She managed to do it without sounding patronizing. "She's doing just fine, really." Sheila smiled at Lori. "Aren't you, Lori?"

Lori felt as if she could hardly draw in enough air to sustain herself. It was leaving her lungs faster than it was coming in. She barely nodded in response to her doctor's question.

"Depends...on...your...definition...of...fine."

The look she gave Lori was nothing if not empathetic. Sheila had two children of her own and knew about the pain of childbirth from both sides of the delivery room. She took a deep breath, as if to brace herself for Lori's ordeal. "Okay, ready?"

Lori wanted to say no, she wasn't ready, but suddenly there was this overwhelming urge to push again and she was swept away with it. She made a noise that passed for agreement.

Behind her, she could feel Carson propping her up again. Offering up quick fragments of all the prayers she could think of, Lori closed her eyes and began to push again.

She was a hell of a lot stronger than he was, Carson couldn't help thinking. He would have been wiped out by the pain. "You can do this, Lori. C'mon, just a little more."

Lori realized that Carson had lowered his head and was uttering the words of encouragement into her ear. They echoed in her head as she bore down a second time, pushing so hard she thought she was going to pass out from the effort.

And then she heard it, heard the tiny wail.

Was that her? Was she making those noises?

No, she realized, the sounds were coming from somewhere else. From her baby.

Her baby.

Lori's eyes fluttered open again and it was like coming out of a deep, gut-wrenching trance.

"Baby?" It took all the strength she had just to utter the single word.

"Baby," Sheila confirmed, pleased. "You have a lovely baby girl with ten fingers and ten toes." She looked up at Lori, beaming.

The nurse beside her took the infant and wrapped her up in a sparkling white blanket. The tiny wail ceased as her huge eyes seemed to sweep around the room, as if she was as amazed to be here as Lori was amazed to finally have her here.

"Would you like to hold her?" Sheila's question was addressed to Carson.

He began to say no, that the joy of being the first to hold this new life belonged to Lori. But one look at the tiny being now nestled against the attending nurse's maternal breast and he knew he was a goner. He fell hard and instantly in love.

Carson looked to Lori for permission. She seemed to understand what he was silently asking her and she nodded her head.

"Yes," he murmured.

The nurse transferred the infant to his arms. They closed protectively around the baby.

The infant was so light, she felt like nothing. And like everything.

Carson had no idea that it could happen so fast, that love could strike like lightning and fill every part of him with its mysterious glow. But it could and it did. It coated him completely, leaving nothing untouched, nothing unaltered.

This tiny life form was deeply embedded in his heart.

"She's beautiful," he told Lori. "But then," he looked at her, "I guess that was a given."

Was that a compliment? Or was her head just fuzzy because of this ordeal? Lori wasn't sure. It wasn't like Carson to say something nice like that, but then, she wouldn't have thought he'd carry her for blocks uphill to the hospital, either.

And then she remembered. "Oh God, Carson, your car."

He'd completely forgotten about that. It had probably been towed away by now. It was going to take some doing to find where it had been taken. He was going to have to call someone to come and get him once he left the hospital. Details, just details. What mattered was that Lori and the baby were all right.

"Good thing we didn't take your car."

Very gently, he lay the infant in the crook of Lori's arm. Stepping back, he looked at mother and daughter and thought that he'd never seen anything more beautiful, never seen Lori looking more radiant. Not even at her wedding to his brother.

Something stirred deep within him, struggling to rise to the surface. Self-preservation instincts had him trying to keep it down, to push it back to where it could exist without causing any complications.

Back to where it had existed all this time without seeing the light of day.

"She has your eyes," he told Lori.

Lori raised hers from her baby's solemn face to his. "And your expression."

"She's young. You'll teach her."

Lori smiled, feeling very content and very, very tired. She looked at him meaningfully. "Yes," she said softly, "I will."

Chapter Eight

They descended upon her en masse, just as they had when they had first gotten together. The ladies of The Mom Squad walked into her single care unit, bearing gifts, good wishes and chatter, all of which Lori welcomed with both arms.

The women were all slender now, living testimony that there was life after pregnancy and delivery. Though she'd espoused the theory time and again for the benefit of the mothers-to-be who populated her Lamaze classes, Lori was genuinely relieved to see it in practice so close at hand. That meant that there was hope for her, too.

Each of the three women hugged her in turn, smelling heavenly and ushering in sunshine.

"Boy," Joanna Prescott, a teacher herself, teased as she stepped back, "leave it to the teacher to be the only one to follow rules and have her baby the prescribed way." She raised a brow. "In a hospital."

Their resident reporter, Sherry Campbell, was more than willing to join in the good-natured razzing. "Not like me, in a cabin almost a hundred miles from a certified hospital."

"Or me," Special Agent Chris "C.J." Jones reminded them, "on the floor of the FBI task office dedicated to tracking down the Sleeping Beauty serial killer."

As far as she was concerned, Joanna felt she had the others beat by a mile. "Oh, and the lawn in front of my burning house was better?"

"Stop." Lori held her hands up to hold back the competitive comparisons. "You're all making me feel deadly dull."

Sherry looked at her in mock surprise. They were all privy to the particulars of the infant's arrival. She, like the other two women, had also met Carson O'Neill the night he'd had to pick Lori up from class because her car was in the shop.

"Oh, I don't know, having a man, who clearly looks like a Greek god, carry you in his arms for five blocks to get to that hospital isn't exactly shabby, you know."

Lori didn't want the women to get the wrong idea. Without looking, they had all managed to find the kind of life partners that most women only dreamed about. But that hadn't happened to her. Carson would probably have been horrified to learn he was cast in that kind of role. "He's my brother-in-law."

C.J. pinned her with a knowing look. "He's a fox," she pointed out.

Lori shook her head. Incurable romantics, all of

them. Including the FBI Special Agent, who should have known better. "You're making something out of nothing."

But C.J. wasn't about to back off. Not when she knew she was right. She'd seen the way Carson had looked at Lori when the latter had been busy answering a question for a straggler. It wasn't the kind of look a brother-in-law directed at his brother's widow. Not unless there was an strong undercurrent of feelings involved.

"I think you're making nothing out of something," C.J. contradicted. As Lori opened her mouth to protest, C.J. added, "Don't forget, it's my job to look beneath the surface. From what I've witnessed, I'd say that the man has definite feelings for you."

Lori sighed. The woman was incorrigible. "Of course he has feelings for me. I'm his late brother's wife and we always got along." She shrugged vaguely. "As far as I know, I'm the only one he's ever talked to about his ex-wife."

Triumphant, C.J. exchanged looks with the other women. "Aha."

She wasn't about to let her thoughts drift that way, no matter how tempting that route might be. "No 'aha,'" Lori told her, "just 'uh-huh.'"

Sherry piled the newly opened gifts that they'd brought together and placed them on the side shelf for Lori. "Sweetie, you pushed out a baby. I really hope you didn't push out your common sense along with her, too."

Lori dug in. "I've always had more than enough to spare."

Sherry's eyes dance. "See that you do," she advised meaningfully. "Nothing worse than slamming the door shut when opportunity comes knocking."

"Opportunity?" Joanna teased. "Is that what you call it now?"

Sherry laughed. "I call it anything it wants to be called. All I know is that if I hadn't gone after that story about Sinjin, I wouldn't have wound up giving birth in his cabin with him acting as a midwife. And, I wouldn't be looking down the right side of a wedding date now."

"That's you, not me," Lori pointed out, then added, "Thank you all for your good thoughts, but you're letting your imaginations run away with you. Carson is just a very good man, that's all."

"Well you know what they say," C.J. told her. "A good man is hard to find and the three of us have just about cornered the market. Carson may be the last of his breed left. I say go for it."

Lori wasn't about to let any latent hopes for any sort of meaningful relationship be nurtured by these women. If Carson occupied a special place in her heart, it was just because he was kind and good and had been there for her when she needed him most. To think anything else was just asking for trouble. She'd had enough of that already.

Lori shifted in her head. "So tell me what's been going on in your lives since we last got together."

It was all the lead-in the others needed.

"I've brought a visitor to see you."

Lori had just begun to drift off. After the Mom

Squad had left, she'd spent the latter part of her morning getting thoroughly acquainted with her brand-new daughter. The nurse had taken the baby away not ten minutes ago, leaving her to take a short nap before lunch arrived.

Carson's voice emerged out of the dream that had begun to form and registered in the back of her mind.

He wasn't in her dream, he was here. In her room. Lori struggled against the curtain of sleep that was surrounding her and forced herself to pry open her eyes.

When she did, she saw Carson walking into the room. He wasn't alone. He'd brought his daughter Sandy with him. At six foot two, Carson towered over the five-year-old who was holding tightly onto his hand.

Lori pressed the top arrow on her guard rail. The back of her bed began to rise slowly until she was sitting up so she could look at her niece. "Hi."

With her thick, straight black hair and electric blue eyes, Sandy O'Neill was a small female version of her father. The little girl smiled shyly at her. Huge, kissable dimples appeared in each cheek.

"Hi," she echoed.

This really was a surprise, Lori thought. She hadn't seen Carson's daughter since Christmas. Jaclyn had given him exactly one day to spend with the little girl. Or, more precisely, six hours. He'd made the most of it. The three of them had shared the time together.

Warm, sweet and quick to laugh, Sandy was everything her mother wasn't. "Have you seen the baby yet?" Lori asked her.

Sandy moved her head from side to side, the tips of her straight bob moving back and forth against her cheeks. Her eyes never broke contact with hers. "No. Daddy wanted to come here first."

"We thought you might want to come with us," Carson explained.

The man continued to be an endless font of surprises. "That was very thoughtful of you."

Carson snorted. "Don't make a big deal out of it," he told her gruffly. "I wasn't sure if I could pick the kid out of the crowd, that's all."

That was a crock and they both knew it. Why was being recognized as a good man so hard for him to accept? "The nurses can always help steer you in the right direction, you know."

"Yeah, well…" Shrugging, he let his voice trail off. He released Sandy's hand, nodding at her instead. "You need help getting up?"

Lori reached for the robe that was stretched out on the end of her bed. Her smile was warm, grateful. "A strong arm to lean on might be nice. By the way, who's taking over my place at the center?"

He doubted that anyone could take Lori's place. She gave a great deal of herself to the kids. A lot more than he was paying her for. "For now, Rhonda's pulling double shift."

Lori thought of the younger woman. "She must be loving that."

"Actually, it's not too bad," he told her. "She just had another big fight with that worthless jerk she's hooked up. They broke up and she has a lot of extra time on her hands. So this is working out."

"Every cloud has a silver lining," Lori murmured, pushing her arms through the sleeves of the robe.

"So you keep trying to tell me," he muttered. The tone of his voice told her that he was no closer to believing that than he'd ever been.

Lori paused to look at him. "Only because it's true." Throwing off the light blanket, she slowly swung her legs down, trying not to allow the pain in her lower half impede her. She scooted to the edge of the bed. "Sandy, can you get my slippers for me?"

The little girl looked eager to be of use. With a solemn face, she crouched down on the floor and elaborately peered under the bed. With a small cry of triumph, she gathered up the slippers and held them against her chest as she stood up again.

"These?"

Lori smiled warmly at her. "Absolutely. But I'm, going to need them on the floor, honey."

"I'll take it from here, Sandy." Taking the slippers from his daughter's hands, Carson placed them on the floor in front of Lori. "Here," he offered, holding out his hand, "just hold onto me."

"Can't Aunt Lori stand up?" Sandy asked, concern pinching her small face.

In response, Lori smiled at the little girl's concern. "I'm just a little wobbly, honey, that's all."

Lori curled her fingers around the hand Carson held out to her. Holding on tightly, she stood up, sliding her feet into the slippers. It wasn't her first time on her feet. Since the delivery, the nurse had been by twice to chase her out of bed and to help her take a short, painful walk down the hall and back to her room. But her legs still felt rubbery and weak.

She was holding on to Carson more than she would have liked. "You might regret this offer," she warned him.

"Let me worry about that." Carson tucked her arm through his, pressing it against his side to anchor her. "We'll take it slow," he promised.

She looked at him for a long moment. "Yes, I know." Her tone was as pregnant as she had been a short while ago.

Carson pretended not to notice. It was easier that way than dealing with the thoughts that kept crowding his head, or the feelings that kept crowding his soul. He looked at her. "Ready?"

She took a deep breath, catching her lower lip between her teeth before saying, "As I'll ever be."

Sandy watched her with wide eyes that were so much like her father's. "What's the matter, Aunt Lori? Are you sick?"

Lori was hanging onto his arm, slightly hunched. "Aunt Lori's got a big hurt," Carson explained tactfully.

"Does it hurt to have a baby?"

"Sandy," Carson warned. He'd told his daughter about the baby being in "Aunt Lori's tummy" because he believed in being as straightforward as possible with her. But he didn't want her asking any probing questions.

"Just a little, honey," Lori lied. She saw Carson looking at her with dubious surprise. "Well, I don't want to scare her," she whispered.

He merely nodded, the corners of his mouth curving slightly.

They had passed the nursery on the way from the elevators. Even at her tender age, Sandy had already demonstrated to Carson that she possessed complete recall. He envisioned a future without limits for his little girl. Dancing ahead of them on her toes, Sandy led the way to the nursery.

She made Lori think of a little fairy princess. Right now, Lori was envious of Sandy's light-footedness. "It was nice of you to bring her," she told Carson.

He took no credit. "I told her about the baby. She wanted to come."

There was more to it than that. He'd told her that his ex-wife was not congenial when it came to visitation rights. "How did you manage to spring her?"

He cut down his stride considerably for Lori's sake. He could feel her digging her fingers into his arm. "Wasn't hard. Jaclyn and her husband left for Hawaii day before yesterday. Sandy was left with the housekeeper."

Who undoubtedly had orders not to let the child see her father, Lori thought. "So you charmed the pants off her."

His laugh was dry, short. "You've got me confused with Kurt. He was the one who could charm articles of clothing off women." A talent that had gotten his brother in trouble more than once. "Besides, Adele is almost sixty," he said referring to the housekeeper. "Her pants are very firmly in place."

"I think you underestimate yourself, Carson. You might not have a golden tongue, but that doesn't make you any less charming or attractive.'' Pausing, she cocked her head as she regarded his profile. ''Joanna Prescott thinks you're a hunk.''

Carson frowned at the assessment. ''Joanna Prescott should have the prescription to her glasses checked,'' he suggested.

''She doesn't wear glasses.''

''Maybe she should start.''

''Oh, I don't know, you do look pretty good in the right light.''

When they were growing up, Kurt had always been the good-looking one. His role had been to be the dependable one. To hear anyone refer to him any other way always raised his suspicions. Carson eyed her now. ''You want me to leave you stranded here?''

She raised her free hand in a mock oath. ''I'll behave.''

He raised a skeptical brow aimed in her direction. ''That'll be the day.''

Sandy was standing on her tiptoes with her face pressed against the large bay window. There were three long rows of bassinets displayed. ''Can we pick out any one we want?'' Sandy wanted to know. She shifted from toe to toe excitedly.

''She's not an ice-cream cone, Sandy,'' Carson told her patiently. ''Each of these babies already belongs to someone.''

Sandy turned partway from the window, looking up at her father. ''Which one belongs to us?''

''The baby belongs to Aunt Lori, not us.''

''We can share her,'' Lori told Sandy with a wink. The girl looked up at her, pleased.

Carson picked his daughter up so that she could have a better view. "It's that one, over there." He pointed out a pink cheeked baby in the third row, the second bassinet from the right end.

From this distance, the name tags were hard to make out. Lori cocked her head as she looked up at him. "I thought they all looked alike to you."

Lori was grinning at him when he looked at her. Putting his daughter down, he shrugged. "She looks more familiar than the others do." He set Sandy down. "Did I guess right?"

Lori looked at him knowingly. "You didn't guess at all."

He supposed there was no point in lying about it. "Yeah, well maybe I was here before. When they put her in her bassinet last night."

She wouldn't have thought he would do that. But then, Carson was doing a lot of things she wouldn't have thought him capable of as little as eight months ago. "You followed the nurse?"

He shrugged. "Just wanted to be sure they didn't lose the kid." Was it his imagination, or did Lori's arms tighten slightly through his?

"Why is it that I never noticed how sweet you were before?"

He didn't have to look at her to know she was smiling. broadly. "Maybe because you were never delirious with pain before."

She took her case to Sandy. "Your daddy's a nice man," she told the little girl.

In response, Sandy turned from the bay window with its large selection of babies that had kept her so fascinated and looked up solemnly at her father. She nodded her head vigorously. ''I know.''

In turn, Lori looked at the man at her side, her point won. ''Out of the mouths of babes.''

He raised a single eyebrow. ''You talking about Sandy or yourself?''

''Scoff if you must, Carson, that doesn't change anything. You're a lot nicer than you want people to know about.''

He merely shook his head. Former lawyer or not, he knew better than to get into a debate with Lori. ''Like I said, delirious.''

The day nurse assigned to the rooms in Lori's section peered into the room. ''Are you all set?''

More than set, Lori thought. She was going home. Barely two days after the delivery and she was going home to begin her life as a mother.

The first step of an eighteen-year journey, she thought.

She glanced down at the suitcase on her bed. Carson had brought it to her the morning after she'd delivered. Except for her nightgown, her robe and the slippers she'd bought expressly for her hospital stay, she hadn't taken out anything. All three items were back in the case.

''All set.''

''Let's not forget the most important item.'' Pushing the door open with her shoulder, the nurse came all the way into the room. Lori's baby was in her arms. ''Can't be a mom without one of these.''

Nerves danced and retreated. Smiling, Lori took the baby into her arms. "No, I guess you can't."

The nurse stood beside her for a moment. She patted Lori's arm. "You'll do fine."

She had her doubts about that, Lori thought, fervently wishing her mother was still alive. For a whole host of reasons. "Can I hold you to that?"

"For as long as you'd like." The nurse adjusted the baby's receiving blanket around her. "Remember, any questions, Blair has a new mom hot line. Night or day, just call," she instructed. "There'll always be someone to answer your questions."

Lori knew that. It was something she told the women at the Lamaze classes. It was something for them to cling to. Now it was her turn, Lori thought. The baby books she'd read were all well and good, but nothing beat talking to someone who had already experienced what she was going through.

"How long am I going to be considered a new mom?"

The nurse smiled at her. "Just until after they go off to college." Taking out a card, she tucked the telephone number into Lori's purse on the table. "Remember, night or day," she repeated. "Now then, who's taking you home?"

"I am."

As if he'd been waiting in the wings for his cue, Carson strode into the room, looking bigger than life to Lori. She smiled a greeting at him. "Hi."

He was running late and there was nothing he disliked more than being late. "There's some kind of construction going on along Blair Boulevard,'' he said by way of explanation.

The nurse nodded, obviously familiar with the problem. ''They've started widening the road.''

Carson frowned. He was a firm believer in not fixing things that weren't broken. ''The road was fine the way it was.''

Lori grinned. ''Don't mind him, he doesn't like progress.''

''I've got nothing against progress. It's gridlock I don't like.'' He paused to look at the baby, then asked Lori, ''You ready?''

She looked around. ''Let me see, suitcase, baby, yes, I'm ready.''

Carson glanced toward the nurse. ''Do I need to sign her out?''

Lori answered for her. ''You're not springing an inmate from an asylum, Carson. You're just taking home a very antsy new mom.''

The word caught his attention. ''Antsy?'' She'd already given birth, what was there to be antsy about? ''Why?''

''Just afraid I'll do something wrong, that's all,'' Lori confessed.

He tried to laugh her out of it. ''That's a first. It never stopped you before.'' Carson grew serious. ''This isn't going to be any different than anything else you've ever done.''

He was supposed to be the pessimist here, not her. ''Since when did you get so blasé?''

He'd done a little attitude adjusting these past few weeks. Circumstances had forced him to do some reassessing. "Since I found out that if life knocks you down, you just have to stand up again."

Taking her elbow, he helped Lori into the wheelchair and then waited until the nurse placed the baby back into Lori's arms. Carson moved behind the wheelchair, taking control. He nodded at the other woman. "Okay, let's roll."

The nurse picked up the vase of flowers that was still in the room. Lori had given away the other flowers, sending them on to the children's ward and to the chapel on the first floor. But the pink and white carnations the nurse was holding had come from Carson. She wanted to take them home with her.

Lori craned her neck to look at him as he pushed her out of the room. "Thanks for coming to pick me up."

"I had to. I was afraid you'd thumb a ride if I didn't." Coming to the elevator banks, he pressed for a car. It arrived almost instantly.

His answer was typically flippant. "Why can't you just let me say thank you?"

He pressed for the first floor. "Had anyone ever been able to stop you from saying anything?"

"You've tried more than once," she pointed out. The passing floors flashed their numbers at them as they went down to the first floor without stopping once.

"Don't remember succeeding, though."

The elevator doors opened. Carson pushed the wheelchair down the long, winding hallway, hardly paying attention to the arrows that guided him to the entrance. He knew the way by heart now.

His car was parked just ahead in the temporary zone. There was a valet standing beside it. "By the way," Carson began as he guided her through the electronic doors. "I'm spending the night."

Chapter Nine

She'd stared at Carson in stunned silence as the nurse momentarily took the baby from her. She continued staring as he helped her out of the wheelchair and into the car. It wasn't until the baby was back in her arms and they had pulled away from temporary loading zone that Lori regained possession of her tongue.

"What do you mean you're spending the night?" She had to have misheard him. "Spending what night where?"

He'd thought he'd been clear enough. Carson glanced at her just before he merged to the left and entered the flow of traffic. "Are you on any medication?"

"Don't change the subject," she warned. "What did you just mean back there?"

Carson frowned as a sports car cut him off. "Same thing I mean here." In deference to the fact that he wasn't alone in the car, he swallowed the curse that rose to his lips. "I'm staying at your house tonight."

The offer had come out of nowhere and it wasn't like Carson. She grinned, wondering if he was aware of how it sounded. "This is a little sudden, don't you think?"

Carson slanted her another look, certain she couldn't mean what he thought she meant. Certain she couldn't be feeling what he'd felt. She was a widow, she'd just given birth and he was the guy who was always just there, that's all.

Wasn't her fault he'd been feeling things lately. That helping her deliver her baby had somehow placed a very different focus on their relationship for him. That her upbeat, warm personality had finally managed to cut through the corrugated fencing he'd kept around his soul. That was his problem, not hers.

But he was more than willing and able to help her with what was her problem. Adjustment.

He winged it. "Sudden? You've been pregnant for eight months. There's nothing sudden about it. I just figured you might need help the first night."

He got that right, she thought. Still, he was the last person she would have thought would realize the fact. The man kept astounding her.

"And you're volunteering?"

He queued onto the freeway ramp. There was some sort of traffic jam on the other side, but except for a few rubbernecks who slowed down to look, their side moved along at a good pace. "Don't see anyone else in the car, do you?"

Just when she thought he was being as nice as he

was possibly able to be, Carson upped the ante. "Just the baby, but she's a little too young to be changing her own diaper," Lori said.

His expression was impassive, unreadable. "Sounds like her mother might be a little too young to change her diapers."

He was covering, she thought. Making a flippant remark about how young she sometimes acted in order to hide something. She wasn't sure what he could possibly want to hide. It couldn't be what she hoped it was. Any excess feelings Carson O'Neill had were all sent special delivery to his daughter. There wasn't anything else left over.

No matter how she was beginning to feel about him.

Because her own feelings were oddly vulnerable now, she retreated to the same flippant ground where he'd taken shelter. "Hey, I've taught men who were all thumbs how to diaper a baby."

She had book knowledge, he had something better. "A doll," he pointed out, "you taught them how to change a doll. The real thing's different." For one thing, it moved a great deal more than a doll did, he thought, remembering his first time. That he'd changed his daughter's diapers wasn't something he'd ever advertised. The information went against the image he liked to project, the one he felt comfortable with. That of an unapproachable authority figure.

But for Lori, he was willing to temporarily abandon that image.

She studied his profile, trying to picture him with baby powder in his hand and a dirty diaper waiting for disposal in front of him. "And you'd know about the real thing?"

His expression never changed. "I've got Sandy, don't I?"

"You diapered Sandy?"

He could hear it in her voice, she was going to start teasing him any second. "What, am I talking a foreign language?"

"Apparently." She knew he wouldn't have revealed this to just anyone and was truly surprised that he trusted her with this information. It touched her. "I just can't picture you diapering a baby, that's all." Her voice became more serious, more thoughtful. "I guess I really don't know you as well as I thought."

He'd never liked the idea of being thought of as an open book. Open books had no privacy and privacy was of paramount importance to him. "There's a lot about me you don't know."

"Apparently," she murmured again.

But she was willing to learn, Lori added silently. More than willing.

The door was open, but Carson knocked anyway. He didn't feel right about just walking in. After all, it was her bedroom and he didn't belong in it.

When Lori turned her head toward him, he told her, "I think the baby's hungry."

Giving in to Carson's insistence, she'd lain down for a few moments. Until she had, she hadn't realized just how exhausted she really felt. This first day was taking more out of her than she'd imagined.

A few moments had easily stretched out into twenty minutes.

Lori sat up, dragging a hand through her hair. She felt guilty about being so inactive. This was her baby and for the past hour, Carson had been the one taking care of her.

Still standing in the doorway, Carson avoided looking in her direction as he explained, "I can't warm up her meal for her."

She was breast-feeding Emma. Lori smiled to herself as she rose. A lot he knew. He'd been warming up the vessel that contained the baby's meal since he'd brought her home. Longer.

Did he even have a clue about the way he'd been affecting her? Would it scare him if he knew? "I'll be right there."

"No need." He walked into the room with Emma. "I brought Mohammed to the mountain."

She laughed, opening the top button of her blouse. "So now I look like a mountain?"

Carson slipped the infant into the crook of her arm, being very careful not to brush his fingers against anything they shouldn't be coming in contact with. "Figure of speech. You don't look like a mountain. You look terrific."

A compliment. Was he even aware he was paying it? She raised her eyes to his. "Really?"

Carson flushed. "I don't say anything I don't mean." As if aware of how close he was to her, he took a step away from the bed. "Just sometimes I say too much."

Her eyes met his. That would be the day. Clams were more talkative than he was. "I don't think so, Carson. God knows no one is ever going to accuse you of being a chatterbox."

He took another step back, then stopped. "I leave that to you."

With the baby pressed against her breast, Lori opened another button on her blouse, and then another. "Thanks a lot."

With effort, he tore his eyes away, although this time it wasn't easy. Noble intentions only extended so far. "Um, I've got some...stuff to see to."

She saw the pink hue creeping up his cheeks. "Are you embarrassed?" Lori stopped unbuttoning her blouse. She'd never thought that anything could embarrass Carson. "You were there at her birth."

"If you recall," he addressed the wall above her head, "I was positioned at your other end."

The man was positively adorable. "And you didn't look?"

"Nope. Figured you needed your privacy, even at a time like that."

She didn't know of any other man quite like him. "You really are amazing, you know that?"

"Like I said," he jerked his thumb toward the hall and beyond, "stuff."

With that, Carson pivoted on his heel and withdrew, moving a little quicker than Lori thought the situation warranted.

The sound of her soft laughter accompanied him out into the hall.

* * *

He was an early riser. He always had been. When he awoke at morning, he was surprised that the baby hadn't interrupted his sleep. Newborns woke up every few hours and made their presence known. He'd fully intended to spell Lori. Instead, he'd slept like a dead man.

Some help he was, Carson thought, disgusted with himself as he made his way into the kitchen. He had every intention of making breakfast for them both.

Entering, he discovered that Lori had gotten there ahead of him. Her back to him, she was just opening the refrigerator.

"What are you doing out of bed?" He wanted to know.

Hurrying, she'd almost dropped the plate of butter she was taking out. She set it on the counter, taking a deep breath to steady her pulse. "I believe it's called making breakfast."

He glanced toward the stove. There was more than enough in the frying pan for two people. This wasn't working out the way it was supposed to.

"I didn't stay over for you to make breakfast for me."

He made it hard to say thank you, Lori thought. "No, you stayed over to see me through my first night and I appreciate that more than you'll ever know." She divided the contents of the frying pan between the two plates she had waiting on the counter. Scrambled eggs filled each. "Now, I can't carry you to a hospital, I can't help you give birth and I can't be your moral support in a time of muted crisis." Placing the frying pan into the sink, she ran hot water into it, then shut it off. "The very least you can do is let me make you breakfast."

He was accustomed to lukewarm breakfasts eaten at his desk at the center. Even when he'd been a lawyer, he'd eaten in his office. "I was thinking of picking up something at a drive through."

Fat, served up medium warm, she thought. The toaster gave up its slices. Moving quickly, she buttered two for him. "Is that how you eat?"

He shrugged. Food was something to sustain him, not something to look forward to. "Most of the time."

"Then I've been remiss." Arranging the toast around his eggs, she placed his plate on the table. "You are hereby invited over for any meal of your choice any time you want." Grabbing a fork and a napkin, she set down both beside his plate. "Now sit."

He was trying to help her cope, not give her more work. "I'm not about to come barging in on you—"

She fixed him with a look. "Sit!"

He didn't feel like getting into an argument first thing in the morning. He planted himself on a chair. "Yes ma'am."

"Better." Taking her own plate, she sat down opposite him in the small nook. There was bacon on her plate. She noticed he looked at it. "I didn't make any bacon for you because I remembered you didn't like it."

They'd never had breakfast together. "How do you know I don't like bacon?"

"Kurt told me." Picking up the curled bacon slice in her fingers, she broke a piece off and popped it into her mouth. "I remember things." A smile curved her lips as she looked at him. "Like that argument we never finished."

He was already sampling his portion. He had to admit, this beat cardboard eggs in a foam box seven ways from sundown. "What argument?"

"More like a discussion, really," she amended, watching his face. "Just before you did your hero thing."

She was talking about that damn fund-raiser, wasn't she? "It wasn't a hero thing and if you want to pay me back for anything, you'll drop the subject."

That far she wasn't willing to go. "You know I'm right."

Why had he even thought she'd give up on this? "What I know is that once you get hold of a subject, you can be a damn pain in the neck about it." She said nothing, merely continued to look at him as she ate. Why did that make him feel like squirming inside? He knew she was wrong about this. "You know, this isn't going to do you any good. I still think it's a bad idea. It's not going to work," he insisted.

"Yes, it will," she countered. Finishing her bacon, she leaned in over the table, her eyes excited. "I already talked to Sherry and Joanna about it when they came to the hospital and they think it's a great idea."

He forced himself to look down at his plate. Looking into her eyes made him lose his train of thought. "Your friends' opinions notwithstanding—"

She knew what he was going to say. That they were

her friends and had to side with her. But that wasn't the point she was trying to make. "And they're both engaged to billionaires."

The information temporarily brought his train to a halt before it could even exit the station. "Billionaires?"

She nodded her head, aware that she'd managed to temporarily derail him. "St. John Adair and Rick Masters. Adair's the head of—"

"I know who he is, who they are." He hadn't been living in a cave, after all. Even if his ex-wife hadn't lived and breathed the society page, the names would have been familiar to him. But even so, he didn't see this half thought out idea of hers taking off. "And these billionaires would be willing to come to a weenie roast at the center."

She ignored his mocking tone. "Your problem, Carson, is that you don't think big. And that you have no faith," she added for good measure. "I also know a caterer. She'd be willing to do this for cost."

Now there was a nebulous word, Carson thought. "Whose cost?"

"It'll be underwritten," she assured him. Either one of the two men's foundations would be more than willing to take on the expense in exchange for the goodwill. "And, I've already developed a theme and everything."

"A theme?" he echoed. What the hell did that have to do with anything?

As if reading his mind, she said, "Can't have a fund-raiser without a theme. Sherry's a former newscaster who's a reporter now," she went on, "and her father is retired from the *L.A. Times,* so publicity is not going to be a problem—"

He leaned back in his chair, looking at her. She'd had a baby less than three days ago. Most women in her position would still be trying to pull themselves together, not pulling together a fund-raiser for high rollers. "You've got this all worked out, don't you?"

She took a bite out of her toast. "All except for you saying yes."

"Does that even matter?" As far as he could see, she was ready to steamroll right over him.

How could he say that? The center was his baby, his domain. She was just trying to help. "Of course it matters." And then she grinned. "It also matters that this'll be written up in the society pages."

"Society pages?" he echoed. Was Lori trying to tell him that she had something in common with his ex-wife? That she craved the limelight, too? "Why should that matter?"

"So Jaclyn can eat her heart out, of course." She knew that he wasn't the vengeful type, but that was all right. She was vengeful for him. "I want her to realize that she lost a catch *and* a chance to come floating in on your arm at a really big charity event."

He laughed, shaking his head. "You're letting your imagination run away with you."

"No, I'm not." She finished her toast. "I just have to have imagination for the both of us, so it seems as if I have too much. What do you say?"

He kept a straight expression. "If I said no—"

She wasn't sure if he was being serious or not.

With Carson it was hard to tell. "I'd hammer away at you until you said yes."

"That's what I thought." Maybe it wasn't such a bad idea after all. Not that part about Jaclyn. He didn't care anymore what the woman thought, only that she was a good mother to Sandy. But the center could definitely use the money. "Let me think about it."

"Really?"

There was something about the way she looked when she widened her eyes like that that got to him. Made his stomach feel like jelly.

Maybe it was time to go. He rose to his feet. "I told you, I never say anything I don't mean."

Lori was on her feet as well. "You won't regret this."

And then, moved by the moment and by everything he'd done that had led up to this point in time, she pulled on his shirt, drawing him down to her level. When he bent his head, a query in his eyes, she raised herself up on her toes and brought her mouth up to his.

He stopped her at the last minute, placing his fingertips against her lips.

Stunned, she looked up at him. Was he rejecting her?

There was a dab of strawberry jam at the corner of her mouth. He slowly rubbed it away with his thumb. His eyes never left hers.

"I know you're a go-getter, but there are some things a man likes to initiate himself. At least the second time around."

He knew he should have just walked away. It would have been the sensible thing to do. But he'd been battling too many emotions lately to be sensible. He cupped her chin in his hand and brought his mouth down to hers.

Carson kissed her with all the feeling that had been churning within him. Kissed her the way he'd been wanting to ever since she'd first kissed him. Ever since, a part of him realized, he'd first seen her on his brother's arm, her eyes sparkling, her manner bursting with the kind of sunshine he had never believed people were capable of exuding.

One look at Lori and he'd been proven wrong.

She tasted of strawberries. He'd always had a weakness for strawberries. And even if he hadn't, he had a feeling that he would have developed one now.

He deepened the kiss, knowing it was a mistake, knowing it would only make him want more. Want her. It was crazy and it was something that he would keep to himself until his dying day, but he knew in his heart that he wanted her.

Wanted Lori not for an hour, not for a night, but forever.

Because even in her stubbornness, she embodied everything he had ever wanted in his life, everything he had ever wanted in a woman. The last bone of contention he'd had with his brother was the way Kurt took Lori for granted.

Had Lori been part of his life, Carson knew he would have never treated her that way, never taken her for granted for even one moment.

But that choice wasn't his. Wouldn't be his.

But if only for the moment, he allowed himself to pretend that it was.

He was making her head spin and her blood rush. She'd never been with another man other than Kurt, but suddenly, she felt as if everything inside of her was being pulled to this man. It wasn't possible, not yet, because strictly physically she wasn't ready.

But that didn't mean that the rest of her wasn't. That the rest of her didn't ache to be his in every sense of the word.

She dug her fingers into his shoulders, trying to steady herself. Wouldn't that be a surprise for him, she thought, to know what she was feeling?

Or maybe, just maybe, it wouldn't be that much of a surprise.

At least, she could hope.

A stab of guilt had him withdrawing. What the hell was he doing, taking advantage of her when she was so vulnerable? What had gotten into him?

"I'd better get going," he murmured. "The center's not going to run itself."

"Carson—"

"Call me if you need anything."

She smiled, watching a six-foot-two man beat a hasty retreat out the door. If she did call him, she thought as she heard the front door closing, it would be because she only needed one thing.

Him.

Chapter Ten

By the time Carson arrived at St. Augustine's, he'd made up his mind. He was only going to call. Just a simple call to check in on Lori and the baby. If even that.

He sat down at his desk, bracing himself for the task he'd put off the past couple of days. Searching for funds to reallocate so that the center's bills could be paid this month. It was a hell of a juggling act.

After all, he argued, his mind slipping back to Lori, he'd already done more than his fair share when it came to helping her out. More than most men would have. He'd filled her refrigerator, brought her home from the hospital and stayed over her first night home with the baby.

Not that she'd really needed him. She'd seemed to manage fine on her own. Just as she'd said.

Just as, he thought, she'd always done.

Maybe it was just his own need to be needed. He

sighed, dragging a hand through his hair. Damn it, he was beginning to sound like one of those afternoon talk shows. Muttering an oath under his breath, he turned his attention back to his unbalanced budget.

No, he wasn't going over tonight, he thought for the hundredth time that day as he regarded the stone-cold, borderline petrified hamburger on his desk. If he couldn't get his mind more than a few inches away from Lori, well that was his problem to deal with, not hers. Things wouldn't improve if he went over.

Besides, Carson shut his eyes, momentarily surrendering the budget battle he was engaged in, he knew if he did show up at Lori's house, she would only start yammering at him again about the fund-raiser. There was no way he wanted to hear any more about that, especially not in his present state of mind.

No, he was going to give her some space. Go home after work and get some well-deserved rest of his own. He'd call her once he got there.

Maybe.

Or maybe he'd just call her now and get it over with. Carson eyed the sickly salmon-colored telephone beside his deceased hamburger, feeling as if he were involved in an exhausting physical tug-of-war rather than just a mental one.

"Hey, boss man." Without bothering to knock, Rhonda swung the office door open and stuck her dark head in. "I think you've got yourself a problem."

That was an understatement, he thought, then realized that she had to be referring to something at the center.

A problem. Good. Something to sink his teeth into. Something to get his mind away from things it shouldn't be dwelling on. Splaying his hands on his desk, he rose to his feet. "Such as?"

She looked unwilling to go into detail. Or perhaps unable. Rhonda wasn't the most articulate person in the world. Not like Lori, he thought. Lori liked to use ten words when three would suffice.

Rhonda nodded toward the hall. "I think you'd better come and see this."

In desperate need of diversion, he still didn't know if he liked the sound of that. But then, Rhonda wasn't the type to tackle things on her own. She was a firm believer in passing on things that she deemed weren't part of her job description.

Not like Lori. Lori tackled everything as if it was her private crusade.

Damn it, O'Neill, give it a rest. The woman's not a saint. What the hell's gotten into you?

He needed a woman, he decided abruptly. Someone to ease the physical tension that had to be at the root of all this. He refused to entertain the idea that there might have been another cause, another solution. Anything that had to do with feelings was going to be left out in the cold.

"What is it?" he asked again. Rhonda led him across the first floor toward the stairwell on the other side of the gym. They cut a wide path around the basketball court.

"One of the guys came and told me that the water

in the boys' shower was cold. I was going to have Juan check that out when Alda told me the same thing was happening in the girls' shower. So I had a hunch and went down into the basement.'' Stopping at the door that led to the basement, she paused significantly.

Carson knew it was because she wanted recognition for her initiative.

Moving in front of her, he opened the door. A long, narrow stairway led down to the basement. It reminded him of something that would have been found back East or up North. For the most part, there were no basements in Southern California. Not in any of the newer buildings. But St. Augustine's Teen Center had originally been an unwed mothers' shelter that had been renovated in the sixties. The building itself was over fifty years old. And not wearing its age well.

''And what did you find there?'' He held on to the rickety banister as he went down the stairs. They creaked under his weight.

''That.'' Rhonda pointed to the inch of water that graced the dirty basement floor. She made no effort to go down the final two steps, the last of which was partially submerged. Instead, she indicated the culprit in the corner. ''Looks like you need a new water heater.''

He bit back a few choice words. Damn, this wasn't going to be cheap. Never mind the cost of the water heater, plumbers were worth their weight in gold.

For a moment, he seriously regretted the altruistic emotions that had caused him to turn his back on the law firm and take up the mantle of shepherd for this dysfunctional flock.

"What was your first clue?" he asked sarcastically.

"The water on the ground."

She was serious. He'd forgotten that humor was something that was usually wasted on Rhonda. Not that there was any in this situation.

Frustrated, Carson dragged his hand through his hair, looking at the mess. Some of the center's gym equipment was stored down here and it didn't take an expert to see that it was ruined.

Well, at least Lori was going to be happy. The thought did nothing to improve his mood. Against his will, Lori was going to get her way. He was going to have to put his faith in a fund-raiser. There was no other way he was going to find any money to repair the damage done by the flood and buy a new water heater.

Not to mention pay this month's electricity bill. Rates had gone through the roof this last year and there was just so much that could be cut back.

When it rained, it poured, he thought. He stared darkly at the dirty water. No pun intended.

She missed him.

There'd been barely two unattended minutes for her to rub together since Carson had left this morning. Visitors had begun dropping by her house within ten minutes of his departure.

But she still missed him.

Not only had each one of the women in the Mom Squad chosen to come by separately to offer encour-

MARIE FERRARELLA 147

agement and advise, not to mention to coo over the
baby, but she'd also received visits from a good many
of the women who had taken her classes and gone on
to have their own babies. Everyone had brought gifts,
food and insisted on spelling her, despite her protests
that she didn't need any "spelling."

News of her delivery had spread quickly and some
of the kids from the center had made the pilgrimage
to her house as well. Angela had been the first and
most enthusiastic. The look in her eyes told Lori that
she'd fallen in love with Emma.

"Gonna have one of these myself one of these
days," she vowed, then looked quickly at Lori and
flushed. "The right way. After I finish school and
after I get me a husband."

She was coming along, Lori thought. "Sounds
good to me."

Angela stayed until her ride came to pick her up
again. The teenager's impromptu visit meant a great
deal to Lori.

But even with this endless parade of hot and cold
running women who insisted on taking over and allowing her to "rest" and not do anything beyond
breast-feed her daughter, Lori found herself missing
him. Missing Carson. Even missing the way he
frowned.

She knew it was futile to feel that way. Carson had
gone more than the extra mile for her and there was
no reason to think that he might come over tonight
for some reason. Now that she had safely delivered
the baby and had been brought to her own home, he
could turn his attention to other important matters.

Without her there to help out, the center was going to take up all of his time. She knew Carson. He didn't believe in half measures.

Or in attachments, she thought as she shut the door on the last of her visitors, holding the baby in the crook of her arm. Carson had made it known to her in no uncertain terms that he was out of the relationship business as far as male and female interactions went.

Though he pretended otherwise, she knew that Jaclyn had hurt him much too much. He'd allowed himself to go out on a limb, to expose himself and become vulnerable and Jaclyn had sawed that limb right out from under him. There was no way he would risk that happening again, Lori thought. She caught a glimpse of herself in the hall mirror. Even with someone who was a great deal more trustworthy than that witch of an ex-wife.

They approached life differently, she and Carson. Kurt hadn't been anything like Jaclyn, but his irresponsibility had eventually worn down the effect of his charm. But she'd discovered that her less than perfect experience with marriage hadn't hardened her heart against further entanglements. It had just made her hopeful that the next one would be *the* one.

If it involved someone like Carson.

''Wouldn't your Uncle Carson just love to hear that?'' she murmured to Emma.

The infant was dozing against her breast. Lori paused for a moment, savoring the silence and just looking at the precious bundle in her arms.

Even after a fair share of dirty diapers and feedings,

it was still hard to believe that Emma was finally here. That the months of nausea, of waiting and worrying were over and that her daughter was finally here, finally part of her life.

"You're every bit as beautiful as I knew you'd be," she whispered to the sleeping face. "But you don't want to hear me carrying on, you want to get your beauty sleep." She began to walk up the stairs. "I warn you, though, you get too much more of that and the princes are going to start lining up at the door fifteen deep. You're not going to know a moment's peace." She grinned. "I suppose there are worse things in life."

Smiling to herself, she walked into the nursery and put the baby down for another nap.

She'd just adjusted the baby monitor when she heard the doorbell.

Was there anyone left in the immediate world who hadn't been by today? She wouldn't have thought so, but apparently there was.

The doorbell rang again before she had a chance to reach the door.

"Who is it?" she called out.

"I brought Chinese this time."

She felt her heart leap up in her chest. The grin spread across her lips instantly. "Carson?"

"Well, it's not the Good Humor Man." The grumpy voice took away all doubt. "Open the door, Lori. These cartons are hot and they're going to break through the bags at any second."

He heard her flipping the top lock. The next moment she threw the door open. The smile in her eyes went right to his gut and made him glad he hadn't talked himself into going home.

"What are you doing here?"

"Trying to bring you dinner." He elbowed his way past her. "Can we play twenty questions later?" Without waiting for an answer, he headed straight toward the kitchen.

She smiled to herself as she closed the door again. Carson was here and everything felt right. "Hello to you, too."

"Hello was implied," he told her curtly, sparing her a short glance over his shoulder. The woman looked better than she had a right to, given the circumstances. In jeans and a tank top, she looked as if she belonged on the cover of a magazine, not someone who had given birth a few days ago.

He forced himself to pay attention to what he was doing and not what he was feeling.

The cartons just barely made it to the counter before the paper bags they were in ripped completely. He took the containers out and bunched up the bags, tossing them into the garbage.

Lori came in right behind him. "You sound like you certainly got up on the wrong side of the chow mein serving."

She took out two soda cans from the refrigerator. Joanna, bless her, had come by earlier with groceries, saying she knew just what it was like, not having a family to fall back on.

Lori popped the tab on the first can and placed it beside a glass for him before repeating the action for herself. She regarded him for a moment. "Anything wrong beyond ripped bags?"

"Yeah," he grumbled, looking down at her. "You're right."

The man certainly liked being enigmatic. The napkin holder was empty. She took out a handful from the pantry and slipped them between the two ends before moving the holder back to the center of the table.

She leveled a look at him. His expression gave her no clue. "I'm right because there's something else wrong, or you're mad because I'm right? Give me a hint here, Carson. Twenty-four hours away from you and I'm getting a little rusty in my Carson-speak."

He sighed, sliding his large frame onto a chair. "You know, I don't know what you're talking about half the time."

Lori gave him a bright smile. "Which means that half the time you do. Always put a positive spin on things, Carson."

She turned away to get two plates out of the cupboard and two forks. She would have taken out her chopsticks, but she knew that Carson was almost hopeless when it came to using them. He'd been nice enough to bring her dinner, she wasn't about to irritate him by flaunting her dexterity. He looked like he had enough on his mind.

"Now," she made herself comfortable at the table, "why are you so extra grumpy?" She thought of the likeliest explanation. "Did something go wrong at the center?"

"Yes."

It was like pulling teeth, but then, that was nothing new. "Are you going to make me guess?" Opening the carton with fried rice, she took out a portion for herself, then passed it on to him. "And if so, how many chances do I get?"

He regarded the carton before him, his expression dour. "The hot water heater broke."

She thought of the old hundred gallon tank. The one time she'd gone into the basement for equipment, the heater had startled her by groaning and making strange noises. "You knew it was only a matter of time, Carson. That thing was ancient."

He passed her the chow mein container. "Yeah, I know."

She knew where this was leading. To a place he was unwilling to go. "Got the money to fix it?" she asked innocently.

"The bottom dropped out," he told her. "It's beyond fixing."

She nodded her head, taking in the information. "Which means you need a new one." She thought of the stack of bills on his desk that he'd been juggling the last month. "Carson—"

He dropped his fork on the plate. "Now you see, that's why I'm angry."

Her expression just grew more innocent. "Because I said Carson?"

She knew damn well that wasn't what he meant. "Because of the way you said Carson."

Lori cocked her head, her eyes holding back a smile. "What way was that?"

"You're going to start nagging again." He looked

at her pointedly. She wasn't saying anything. "About that fund-raiser."

Lori turned her attention to the meal. "Nope, not me. I'm done nagging."

He looked at her incredulously. Lori might as well have said that she'd just died and gone to heaven. He figured it would take that much for her to desist. "You're done nagging," he repeated.

"Absolutely." She was innocence personified as she looked at him. "Well, it hasn't done any good, so there's no point in getting on your nerves. You're an adult, you'll figure a way out of this without my putting in my two cents."

"So that's it?" He didn't believe her, not for one second.

She savored the forkful of sesame chicken she'd slipped between her lips. He'd remembered her favorite, she thought. The man just kept on amazing her. "That's it."

"You're going to stop talking about the fund-raiser." He was waiting for a contradiction.

Her blue eyes were causing his stomach to tighten even though they were doing nothing more than talking about raising money for the center.

She raised her hand in a solemn oath. "Not another word."

Carson frowned. That wasn't the way he'd wanted to play it. He'd wanted her to push her cause and then, after some wrangling, he'd give in. He didn't want to just surrender without her laying siege to him.

But she left him no choice. His back was against the wall and it was either this or begin bankruptcy proceedings. He wasn't about to let that happen before he exhausted all other avenues.

He didn't like this avenue.

Carson blew out an angry breath. "All right, you win."

"Win?" she echoed, a smile playing along her lips. She fluttered her eyelashes. "What do I win, Carson?"

He realized she'd been putting him on. That didn't change the course of the conversation. "We'll have the fund-raiser. It goes against everything I believe in to go out there with my hat in my hand, but there's no other way."

She was delighted at the turn of events. She could finally be of some kind of real help to him.

"No hat in hand, Carson, I promise. When we get through with them, they'll be begging to give you money." Her appetite on hold, she pulled the pad over from the edge of the table. Her eyes were shining as plans began forming in her mind. "We still need a theme." It took her only a second. Her eyes were gleaming as she announced, "I know, we'll have a fifties party."

This was already beginning to sound bad to him. "What?"

"The center was built in 1951," she reminded him. "You know, the era of the poodle skirt, slicked back hair and innocence—" She winked. "Or so they tell me."

"Why do we need a theme?" Even when his life had been on an upward swing and he'd been part of the firm, he'd always opted for simplicity.

"Two reasons. People like a worthy cause and people like having an excuse to dress up and have a good time." She knew what he was going to say and cut him off. "I know, not you, but most people. Anyway, we'll give them both."

"What 'we'?" His part in this, he thought, was just to give Lori her lead. "This is going to be strictly your operation."

"You make it sound like the invasion at Normandy." She made a few notes to herself. "This is going to be fun, Carson." She saw the dubious look on his face. "Trust me."

"I won't have to dress up, will I?" He didn't like the way her grin widened. He pushed back his plate. "Oh no, count me out. You run this whole thing. I'll be the invisible partner."

"Silent," Lori corrected. "Not invisible." She pushed his plate back toward Carson. "You have to be there."

This was going to be her show. She was doing it for the center. There was no need for him to even show up. "Why?"

"Because St. Augustine's is your center. I promise, you won't have to do anything but dress yourself." She winked at him again, sending off strange ripples through him. "I'll do everything else."

The thought of her dressing him suddenly flashed across his mind, causing havoc in his system before he shut it away. "You just had a baby. You're tired."

She put her own spin on it. "I just shed some baby weight, I'm energized."

He sighed, shaking his head. "I was afraid you'd say that."

But he couldn't quite get his voice to sound as disgruntled as he wanted it to. He knew he hadn't succeeded when he saw the pleased smile on her face. The vague thought that it was worth the price whispered across his brain before he had a chance to block it.

"Okay," she was saying, passing him an egg roll. "Let's get our guest list together."

"And she's off," he murmured.

The look she gave him curled through his belly and went straight to places that should have been left out of this.

He bit down hard on his egg roll.

Chapter Eleven

Carson stood staring at the outfit that Lori had left hanging on the inside of her hall closet door. She'd directed him to it as she went back into the guest room to put on her own costume for tomorrow's fund-raiser. She wanted him to see her in it.

There was a red jacket, faded jeans and a white T-shirt hanging in front of him, daring him to try them on. He glanced over toward the guest room. "You're kidding, right?"

Her voice came floating out of the room. "What's the matter, don't you like it?" She didn't give him a chance to answer. "Try it on, you'll look like James Dean. Or what he might have looked like if he hadn't died in that car accident."

"If he hadn't died in that car accident, he'd be an old man now."

He heard her sigh. "Then," she corrected. "The way he'd looked back then."

Carson picked up the red windbreaker's sleeve and shook his head. She couldn't be serious.

As if reading his thoughts, Lori called out, "You're not playing along, Carson. The fund-raiser has a fifties motif, remember?" She paused a second and he knew she was thinking, always a dangerous thing as far as Lori was concerned. "Would you rather dress up like Cary Grant in *Mr. Lucky* or *Houseboat?* That might be more your style, although the outfit is less recognizable. Dressed like that, you'll just be a man in a tux. Everyone's pretty much familiar with James Dean's jeans and red windbreaker from *Rebel Without A Cause.*"

That was just the trouble. He didn't want to look like an idiot, emulating a man who'd been dead for over forty-five years. "What are you wearing?" he wanted to know. "A poodle skirt and a sweater set?"

"Not quite."

Lori stepped out of the guest room. Carson's tongue was suddenly in danger of sliding down his throat.

She was wearing a white sundress that seemed to be a flurry of soft white pleats that caressed her curves with every move she made. The halter top showed off her shoulders to their advantage and his disadvantage. They displayed more white, creamy skin than he felt safe being around. Her legs were bare and she was wearing white, sling back high heels. Lori's light blond hair was teased and fashioned in a classic, familiar style that had been a sex goddess's trademark in the fifties. She even had a beauty mark near the corner of one side of her mouth.

Lori held out the skirt and twirled around one complete revolution for his benefit, her eyes barely leaving his face. "So, what do you think?"

He'd never been one for movies, but he knew what he liked. "Damn."

She smoothed down the skirt. The outfit made her feel just this side of wicked. So did the look in his eyes. Whether he knew it or not, he made her feel like a woman again. "Good damn or bad damn?"

"Just damn," he breathed, grateful that he still could. "You look like—"

Knowing his limited range when it came to movie stars, she came to his rescue. "Marilyn Monroe in *Seven Year Itch,* I hope."

"Better." The halter accentuated her breasts and dipped down low. Realizing he was staring, Carson looked down at her waist. It was as slender as it had been the day she'd married Kurt. "Nobody'd ever guess you just had a baby."

Dimples flashed as she grinned. "Unless I forget to use her drool cloth just before I go." She crossed to the closet where his costume was still hanging. "So, what'll it be? Cary Grant or James Dean?"

Carson frowned. He hadn't even had a suit on since he'd left the law firm. He passionately disliked getting dressed up and donning a costume was even worse.

He closed the closet door, hoping to end the discussion. "Couldn't I just be me? Nobody's going to look at me anyway, not if we walk in together."

Did he even realize what he'd just said? Probably not. "Why, Carson, that just might be the nicest thing you ever said to me."

Feeling uncomfortable, he shoved his hands into his pockets. "I must have said something better than that to you."

"Not that I recall." Moving him aside, she opened the closet door again. This time, she took out the costume and draped it across the back of the sofa. "But don't try to turn my head with compliments, I'm determined to get you into the full swing of this." She regarded the costume, then looked back at Carson, trying to picture him in it. "Now, if you want that tuxedo, I can probably scare one up for you, but you have to tell me now. We don't have much time."

She didn't have to tell him that. The fund-raiser's date had haunted him ever since he'd given her the green light three weeks ago. He'd never seen a woman work so hard so quickly. You would have thought that just adjusting to being a new mother would have been enough for her to handle.

"And everyone's coming." He still couldn't believe it. A hundred and fifty people had been invited to this wild scheme of hers. She'd even invited the other lawyers who had been part of his firm. He'd found that out when one of the senior partners had called in person to confirm. He'd almost called the whole thing off then, but one look at Lori's radiant face as she went over plans with him had made him swallow his words before they'd ever had a chance to emerge.

She nodded. "According to their RSVPs, everyone's coming." Picking up the red windbreaker, she held it up against Carson. She liked the way it made him looked. Sexy, wild. "Actually, with Sinjin and

Rick Masters coming, we could opt for an intimate party of eight and still get enough money to keep you going for the next few years."

Each of the two men had already separately let her know that they were more than willing to make generous contributions to the center, as well as lend their names to the function, thereby guaranteeing its success. It certainly did help to have connections, she mused.

"But the object of this little shindig," she said before he pounced on her comment like a drowning man grabbing a lifeline, "is to get the center solvent for many years to come. Not to mention getting a few computers and a new roof for the place."

The roof had been her addition last week. New computer was a brainstorm that came two days ago. He pushed aside the windbreaker. "Why is it that every time I talk to you, the center's wish list has grown?"

She placed the jacket back on the sofa beside the jeans and T-shirt. "Because I keep thinking of things that would be useful at the center." She'd already told him this part, but she saw no harm in repeating it. In typical male fashion, he probably hadn't been listening the first time around, anyway. "If we had a class teaching them basic computer skills, those kids could get decent jobs and maybe save up some money so they could get into college when they graduated. To have that kind of a class, we need computers. And as for the roof, have you taken a look at it lately?"

"Yes, I have," he said curtly. Patching had all but reached the end of its usefulness. They needed a new one. The last Santa Ana winds had seen to that. "Anything else on your wish list I should know about?"

She was standing toe-to-toe with him, very aware, suddenly, of his maleness. And of the fact that she was very, very attracted to him. "I wish you were more flexible, but that's something I can't buy."

He touched her hair and was surprised to discover that it wasn't stiff with hair spray. It felt silky against his hand. He found himself tangling his fingers in it. Tangling his soul in hers.

"Maybe you could trade for it."

She tilted her face up to his. "What would you like to trade?" she asked in a low whisper.

He had no idea where that had come from or why he'd even said it. Maybe it was the perfume she was wearing. Or the way she looked like pure sin. Or the way she looked up at him, her eyes tempting him to abandon caution. To take another risk.

It was playing havoc on his thought process. On his desire.

"Let me think on it," he murmured just before he brought his mouth down to hers.

Every time he kissed her, it was easier to let go of his resolve not to. Each time he kissed her, he was more tempted than before to continue kissing her. To turn his back on everything he'd promised himself he would never do again.

He felt himself aching again. Needing again.

Warm waves of desire passed over Lori, drowning her. Thrilling her. She stood on the very tips of her toes and wrapped her arms around his neck, drawing her body against his. Savoring their closeness.

His heart was pounding as their lips drew apart. "Damn, but you make it hard, Lori."

She felt just the slightest bit fuzzy, just the slightest bit deliciously dazed. Her eyes searched his face. "What do I make hard, Carson? What?"

His hands were on her shoulders. It was himself that he was holding back, not her. "You make it hard for me to remember that you're my brother's wife."

That was still between them and it shouldn't be. "Widow, Carson, I'm your brother's widow, not his wife. Not any longer. And why do you need to remember that?"

Didn't she understand? "Because this shouldn't be happening. I shouldn't feel this way."

Feelings, he had feelings for her. Something inside of her sang. She could feel her pulse accelerating. "How, Carson, how do you feel? Tell me."

Her question undulated along his skin, along his mind. Like a siren's song, leading him to places that were far too dangerous for him to navigate around.

He had to leave. Now. Before he couldn't.

He didn't.

"Like this," he murmured against her mouth a moment before he kissed her again. Kissed her with a passion that broke through the steel bands he had wrapped around it.

He could feel his blood surging through his veins, could feel it roaring in his ears. Could feel his head spinning as he closed his eyes and let himself go, just for a moment.

No more than that, just for a moment.

Because a moment was all he could safely risk. Any longer and he knew that he would lose all control. Lose himself in her.

And that would be a very dangerous thing to do.

He wanted her. Wanted to make love with her. Wanted to feel her soft skin yielding itself up to him.

Too far, this was going to far.

With superhuman control, he reined himself in. Carson released her shoulders and drew his head away. "I'd better go."

Something inside of her felt like weeping, but she made an effort not to show it. "So, is it James Dean or Cary Grant?"

He shrugged. "You've already got the costume. It might as well be James Dean."

She grinned. Taking the jacket, jeans and T-shirt, she hung them up again in the closet. "Always knew you were a rebel at heart."

That wasn't all his heart was, Carson thought grudgingly as he let himself out.

She was in her element, Carson thought the next evening as he watched Lori work the festively decorated ballroom of the Grand Hotel.

Lori might have a degree in digital design, might be an aide at the center and teach Lamaze classes at Blair Memorial, but she was a born hostess. A born charmer.

Like Kurt, he remembered. Except that in her case, Lori used her gift to help others, not just to be self-serving. Once she'd broken him down and he'd agreed to having the fund-raiser, she'd taken off like a lit Roman candle, illuminating everything within her scope.

True to her word, she'd handled everything, the invitations, the catering, the sponsors. All she'd required of him was his presence and his tolerance. The latter involved wearing tight jeans and a jacket whose color would have never been even his fiftieth choice. But she had thrown herself into this so hard, he felt he couldn't really turn her down, even though he would have preferred spending the evening in the solitude of his home, waiting to have her come by and tell him how it went.

No, that wasn't quite true. He did enjoy being here, he had to admit, but only because it allowed him to watch her work the room.

Allowed him to watch her move like every man's secret fantasy, her slender hips moving just enough to undo every single man within eye range.

Well, maybe not every man. Masters, Adair and that special agent he'd been introduced to, Byron Warrick, all looked to be taken with the women who had accompanied them to this fund-raiser, but he'd noticed more than one man stare after Lori with a note of longing whenever she walked by. Her Marilyn Monroe outfit had only a little to do with it.

It made him feel possessive.

It made him feel, Carson realized with a start, jealous.

As if she was his to be jealous of, he admonished himself Anything she might feel for him was obviously just tangled up with gratitude. He knew that.

She'd been in a bad place when Kurt had been killed and he'd come through for her. It would have been against his nature not to.

The danger here was getting caught up in the woman's smile. In the woman herself.

"Smile," she said, coming up behind him. "You're supposed to be having a good time."

The warm flush that went over him took a bit of doing to hide. "I am." He picked up a glass of white wine from a passing waiter and took a sip to prove his point. "Can't you tell?"

He wasn't fooling her. She'd watched him hang back all evening and had all but dragged him over when the press photographer had taken his pictures. "I've seen people looking happier in a dentist's waiting room, queuing up for a root canal."

"Just my way, Lori, you know that." He took another sip of the wine. He didn't usually care for wine, but this was surprisingly appealing. Or maybe it was just Lori going to his head. "You did a good job."

She looked around the large room. People looked to be enjoying themselves. And happy people were generous people. "It did turn out pretty well, didn't it?"

There was no vanity in her assessment, he noted, only pleasure. It occurred to him how terribly different she and his ex-wife were. Jaclyn would have been looking to get herself into every photograph, mentioned in every line of press.

For the first time, he noticed that Lori had a small drawstring purse hanging from her wrist. She held it up in front of him. "And I've gotten a lot of checks and pledges for the center." She was very, very pleased with herself "We can afford twelve new water heaters and five roofs, stacked one on top of each other."

In general, he disliked exaggeration. Hers only succeeded in amusing him. "We'll just need one of each."

She threaded her arms around his free one. "Well, then we're going to have a great deal of money left over for a lot of other necessary things. The center's going to be giving computer classes," she suddenly remembered to tell him. "Sinjin's seeing to that personally." She waved as the man and Sherry looked in her direction. "One of the companies he owns manufactures computers."

The woman was nothing short of incredible. She'd only thought of the idea a few days ago and already it was a reality. "The kids are going to think you're some kind of fairy godmother."

Turning toward him, she shook her head. "No magic, Carson, just kind hearts. Like I've always told you, people are basically good if you just give them a chance to be."

He'd been raised on the same mean streets that also housed St. Augustine's. His father had abandoned his family and everything he'd ever gotten he'd had to struggle for. And when he'd grown up, he'd dealt with all manner of criminals who needed representation. In addition, when he'd tried to bring meaning to his life, his wife had left him to look for someone with more promise and more money.

He shook his head. "Sorry, I'm afraid I never saw

things that way. My world isn't exactly what you'd call rosy.''

Why did he always insist on painting everything in such dark hues? ''You help kids who might have been hopeless if you hadn't come into their lives, what's rosier than that?''

''You.''

He was doing it again, making her feel all warm inside. If she didn't know that it would embarrass him, she would have kissed him right there, in front of everyone. Instead, she just laughed.

''Well, that goes without saying.'' Taking his glass from his hand, she took a tiny sip. ''Just one,'' she told him when she saw the surprised look that came into his eyes. She gave him back his glass. ''For energy. There's still half a room to schmooze with.'' She looked at him, extending her hand. It would be so much better if he was at her side. ''Come with me.''

But he just shook his head. ''I'd only get in your way.''

She knew better than to push. With a sigh, she nodded. ''Have it your way.''

''That'll be a first.''

She left him with a smile. But she was back in a few minutes. The band was beginning to play another set. ''I need to take a break,'' she told him. ''Dance with me, Carson.''

''I don't dance, you know that.''

She was quick to contradict him. ''You don't dance fast dances.'' She presented her hands to him. ''This is a slow dance. You dance slow dances. I've seen you.''

''When?'' he challenged. He couldn't remember the last time he'd been anywhere with music.

''At my wedding. With me. Remember?''

He remembered. Remembered thinking that he had never seen anyone looking so radiant. ''But not since then.''

''It's like riding a bike.'' She threaded her fingers through his. ''It'll come back to you, I promise.''

''And if I step on your foot?''

She turned her face up to his, already swaying against him. ''I won't sue. Can't get a better deal than that, Counselor.''

''I suppose not,'' he allowed grudgingly.

She felt good in his arms. Too good. He let his mind drift again, fueled by a desire that had no place in their relationship, not even fleetingly. What did it take to get that through his head?

Apparently a lot more than it was taking now, he thought, inhaling the scent in her hair as she laid her cheek against his shoulder.

''Were Marilyn Monroe and James Dean ever an item?''

He felt her smile against the T-shirt, a warmth spreading through his chest on point of contact. ''Not that I know of. Why?''

''No reason. Just wondering.''

That showed a glimmer of imagination. He was coming along. Tiny, baby steps, she thought, but he was coming along. It was all she asked.

* * *

"I feel giddy," Lori told him, closing the door as Diane Jones departed. C.J. had insisted on lending her her mother as a baby-sitter for the evening. She had to admit she'd felt better leaving her daughter in such competent hands. Mrs. Jones had raised five children of her own. "Must be my second wind."

"Or your twelfth." She looked at Carson quizzically as she slipped out of her shoes. The woman was positively tiny, he thought. Like an ounce of dynamite. "I never saw anyone with as much energy as you have." It was two in the morning and by his count, Lori had worked almost round the clock today, supervising and getting everything ready for the event. "A dozen other women would have been exhausted by now."

"You mean a man wouldn't have been exhausted in my place?" There was amusement in her eyes.

"No, I always thought of women as the heartier breed." He unzipped his jacket. "And the deadlier one."

She saw the look in his eyes. "You're talking about Jaclyn, aren't you?"

He shrugged out of the windbreaker, tossing it on her sofa. He didn't want to go there tonight. "Just making a comment, that's all."

She didn't dislike many people, but she disliked Jaclyn for the way she'd hurt Carson. Disliked her with a passion. "Not all women are like Jaclyn, Carson."

It didn't matter one way or the other. "I'm not planning on running a survey."

She looked up at him. "I wouldn't think you'd have to."

"No," he agreed, cupping her cheek, "I don't."

He was sinking again, he thought, sinking into her eyes. Getting lost again. He had to be stronger than that. They had something good right now, something he enjoyed. He didn't want to ruin it by trying for anything more. Half of something was better than all of nothing.

"Lori, I don't think we should let anything happen."

Too late. "I'm sorry, Carson, I'm not as regimented as you are. I can't pencil in feelings. Or pencil them out. They just happen." And they had happened to her. Because of him.

He had to stop it now, before he did something even more stupid than he'd already allowed himself to do. Before he started kissing her and never stopped. "Well, maybe they shouldn't."

He looked troubled, she thought. And there was a panicky feeling taking a toehold inside of her. She needed help in banking it down. "Talk to me, Carson. What's wrong?" *What's wrong with us getting closer?* she wanted to cry.

She looked sad. Vulnerable. He wanted to stay and comfort her, but he knew that would be both of their undoing. He was perilously close to crossing a bridge that allowed no way back.

He had to leave before he couldn't.

Carson backed away. "Look, it's late and the baby's going to be waking up soon. You should get some rest."

"Fat chance," she muttered, staring at the closed door through the tears in her eyes.

Chapter Twelve

Lori paced the floor restlessly, unable to sleep. The clock on the nightstand was serenading 1:00 a.m. Emma was asleep in the next room and so should she be, but she couldn't. Hadn't been able to sleep for several nights now.

It was all Carson's fault.

He hadn't been over in a week. Not since the night of the fund-raiser. At work, it was as if they had suddenly become strangers. That was the way he was treating her. Politely, distantly. As if they hadn't just been on the brink of something far more meaningful, far more intimate.

And it was driving her crazy.

She had no idea how to approach him, how to scale this new glass wall that had appeared without warning between them. She could see him, but she couldn't touch him. Couldn't even make him smile.

Why?

Exasperated, she went downstairs to the kitchen. Maybe warm milk would soothe her, although she didn't hold out much hope.

She took out the carton and poured a glass, then placed it into the microwave. She set the dial for forty-five seconds, then pushed the start button so hard, the oven moved back on the counter.

Had they gone too far for him? That night of the fund-raiser, when he'd brought her home, had there been too many charged emotions between them? Had he suddenly withdrawn because the risk of what was ahead seemed too great for him to take?

The microwave dinged and she yanked the door open. Some of the milk spilled over the top. She mopped it up with a sponge and a sigh.

Damn it, if she was willing to venture out, why wasn't he? Risks were taken every day. It was a risk to leave the house every morning, to cross the street. Some people never made it back. Most did. Why couldn't he think that way?

The odds were in their favor. But only if they tried. *He* had to try.

She took a sip of the milk and burnt her tongue. With disgust, she poured out the rest in the sink.

He wasn't trying. And she was tired of doing the work for both of them. It wasn't the work she minded, it was getting summarily rejected that hurt. And continued to hurt.

Lori pressed her lips together. Drastic times required drastic measures. She'd done everything she could to be encouraging, now it was time to try something else. There was only one thing left as far as she could see.

She hadn't wanted to do this, but he left her no choice. She had to risk everything.

And perhaps be left with nothing.

But she didn't know what else to do.

Carson sat outside on his patio, looking up at the same full moon that was keeping Lori company. Though he had no way of knowing, the same sleeplessness dogging him that afflicted her.

He'd been keeping himself so busy, you'd think he'd be able to sleep at night when there should have been nothing left but exhaustion to tuck itself around him.

But he couldn't. And that was because there was something else besides exhaustion haunting him. There was Lori. His desire for Lori. Each day, it loomed a little larger, a little more prominent, and he hadn't a clue what to do about it.

It scared him, pure and simple.

He wasn't a man who scared easily. Carson liked to think of himself as someone who faced all of life's challenges head-on without flinching. And he had. So far.

But this, this was something different. This involved not risking his body, but his heart and that organ had sadly proven to be too fragile a thing to survive without layers of protection to keep it safe.

Even so, it had succumbed.

To her.

There was no kidding himself. All manner of arguments to the contrary, he was in love with Lori. Very much in love with Lori. And he knew where that path led. He'd only ventured out on it once and had been badly beaten back for his trouble. He wasn't any good at it. At relationships.

The scars had finally healed. This time. But what of the next time? What if he told Lori what was in his heart and she looked at him with pity? What if she didn't feel what he felt? Things would never be the same between them.

Or what if they gave it a try and the romance led nowhere? He didn't think he could endure the disappointment of that. Or of losing her in his life because he knew he would. Friends who turned into lovers never remained friends once the romance was over, no matter what promises they made to each other.

He didn't want to lose her.

It was better this way, nothing ventured, nothing gained.

Nothing lost.

Sitting behind his desk, Carson stared up at Rhonda. The words she'd just said in response to his question felt as if they had bounced off his ears without entering, without being absorbed.

For one small second, he felt confined, as if his office had suddenly turned into a coffin, sealing him into a tiny space.

After more than a week of playing hide and seek, of being everywhere Lori was not, he needed to talk to her. The computers for that class she was so keen on starting for the kids at the center had arrived. Since this was her baby, he couldn't just let the moment pass without interacting with her. Feeling that it was better to be in her company with someone else there, he'd asked Rhonda to have Lori come in.

Only to be told that it wasn't possible.

He had no idea why, but he had a bad feeling when the aide said the words to him. "Why? Didn't she come in today?"

Rhonda shoved her hands into her back pockets as she shook her head. "No."

For someone who loved to gossip, Rhonda was being oddly uncommunicative. "Well, did she call in sick?"

"No." Digging further into one pocket, she pulled out a wrinkled envelope. "She gave me this last night to give to you."

"Last night?" he echoed. Carson looked at the envelope she held in her hand. The bad feeling intensified. "Then why didn't you give it to me?"

"She made me promise I wouldn't give it to you until you asked about her." Rhonda put the envelope down on his desk. "She said she didn't think it would be for a few days."

That was crazy. "What, she thought I wouldn't notice she wasn't here?"

Rhonda raised her model-thin shoulders and then let them drop again carelessly. But her eyes were boring small, accusing holes into him. "That's what she said."

Carson muttered something unintelligible under his

breath as he tore open the envelope. The paper inside had only two sentences written on it: You win. I quit.

He stared at the words as if they were gibberish. Slowly, they finally registered in his brain. Was this some kind of a new game Lori had decided to play? "She says she quits."

"Yeah, I know." Rhonda rocked on the balls of her feet. Her tone told him that she'd been confided in while he had not. "Does this mean you want me to work more hours? Because I could use the raise in pay—"

He didn't want to talk about more hours, or pay raises. His brain felt as if it was suddenly under siege and a cloudy mist had encircled it. He waved her away. "I'll get back to you."

He wasn't even sure just when Rhonda withdrew. Maybe then, maybe a few minutes later. He just sat looking at the almost pristine piece of paper. The words in the center of the page were cold, austere. Lori hadn't even put down a reason.

Anger bubbled up within him, but he banked it down. He shouldn't be angry, he should be relieved. This was, he told himself, for the best. Because he didn't know how much longer he could continue to do the right thing. If their paths kept inevitably crossing, as they would at work, he knew it was only a matter of time before he did something stupid again.

Before he gave in to the ache that had become his constant companion and risked everything.

Possibly to be left with nothing.

He'd done that before, risked everything, but it had

been for a noble reason. He'd risked everything to help the kids at the center. And he'd wound up losing a wife in the bargain.

One risk was enough in anyone's lifetime.

He was just going to have to remember that.

Very slowly, Carson opened his middle drawer took out a manila folder. He slipped Lori's abbreviated letter of resignation into it.

Then filed it away.

That was that.

He slammed the drawer a little harder than he meant to.

He thought it would be better, but it wasn't. It just got worse.

Not having Lori around, knowing she wouldn't *be* around, only made the longing within his chest more acute. Nothing staved it off.

Nothing interested him. Not even working on the '54 Buick Skylark he'd been lovingly restoring in his garage every free moment he could spare. Working on it had seen him through his divorce. He'd thrown himself furiously into its restoration when Kurt had died. It had kept him sane then.

But not now. Nothing was working now. Not his visits with his daughter, who asked about Lori and the baby incessantly, not his job, not the Skylark. Nothing.

Throwing down the rag he'd used to polish a section of the passenger door, Carson went to get his car keys. He knew what he had to do.

* * *

Someone was leaning on her doorbell. Not ringing it, leaning on it. Turning the baby monitor up as she left the kitchen, she hurried to the front door.

The last person in the world she expected was standing on the other side.

Carson was wearing faded, paint-splattered jeans that had holes at each of the knees and a T-shirt that was torn in two places. He looked like a brooding rock star in search of a groupie and the right, elusive lyric.

"I never knew a human being could be so miserable and still live."

She willed her pulse to return to normal as she closed the front door. Part of her had given up hope that he would ever turn up. It had been over three days since she'd handed in her resignation.

"Exactly what are you talking about?"

He turned on his heel, almost bumping into her. "Why aren't you at work?"

She lifted her chin defiantly. "Don't you remember? I quit."

Yes, he remembered she quit. Quit the center, quit him. Nothing else had been on his mind for the past seventy-two hours. He'd lifted up the phone to call her so many times, he'd almost developed carpal tunnel syndrome in that hand.

His eyes narrowed as he looked at her. "What are you doing for money?"

So that was it, he was still playing big brother? She didn't want a brother anymore, she wanted the man who had kissed her, who'd made her feel that there was something more for them. "Don't worry about me."

"What are you doing for money?" he repeated. He knew her finances were shaky. Kurt hadn't left her with anything but bills.

Her voice became icy, distant. "Sherry showed Sinjin some of my work and he asked me to handle the Web pages for his companies. The money's excellent and I can work out of the house most of the time, be around the baby. Everything's perfect," she fairly snapped.

Everything was perfect for her. Not so perfect for him. He was dying inside the way he never thought he could. He played the only card he felt he had. "The kids at the center miss you. And Sandy misses you."

And you? What about you? Can't you even tell me that much? "And I miss them and her," she said tersely. "I can volunteer some time on Sundays at the center." As to Sandy, she had no solution there, even though she loved the little girl as if she were her own. His time with his daughter was limited, she wouldn't very well tell him to drop Sandy off at her house and come back for her later.

Was she that determined to keep away from him, to severe all ties? He had no idea until now how much knowing that could hurt. His voice was very still as he said, "I'm not around on Sunday."

"Exactly." Her chin went up even more pugnaciously, daring him to say something. "Isn't that the way you want it?"

"No."

She had no idea what he meant, what he was thinking. Her intuition had completely deserted her.

"Then how *do* you want it, Carson? Because I'm tired of guessing. Tired of being slapped down." Her voice rose, crackling with all the emotion she was attempting to suppress. "Yes, that's right, Pollyanna has her limits, too. And getting pushed away a hundred and twelve times is mine."

Carson looked at her stonily. "It hadn't been that often."

"Damn it—" she threw up her hands, moving away from him before she did something she'd regret "—I'm exaggerating the number, not the situation. The way I always do. You'd think you'd know me by now."

He caught her by the shoulders and spun her around, forcing her to face him.

"I do," he said fiercely. "I know everything about you. I know the way your eyes light up when you have an idea, or when you've made someone come around. I know the way you laugh. High when something's funny, low when it's at yourself." His eyes searched her face, trying to see if he was getting through, if she understood what he was telling her. "I know the sound of your walk when you're coming down the hall at the center. Like harnessed energy just waiting to go off. I know the curve of your mouth when you smile. It's like sunshine, brightening everything it touches."

There was nothing but stillness for a long moment. She blew out a breath. "Well, you certainly do know the way to take the wind out of someone's sails."

He wanted to take her in his arms, to hug her to him, but he was afraid. Afraid that it was too late. So he stood there, still holding her shoulders, still searching for signs.

"I don't want to take the wind out of your sails, Lori. And I don't want to be adrift again. I thought I could back away, for both our sakes. But I can't." Suddenly aware that he was still holding her in place, he dropped his hands helplessly to his sides. "Nothing's right without you. Nothing fits anymore. Not my purpose, not my skin, nothing."

She was almost afraid to breathe. "So what are you saying?"

He felt like a drowning man, still searching for something to keep him afloat. "I was hoping you'd say it for me."

She wasn't going to make it easy for him. She had before, but if there was ever going to be anything for them, it had to be his turn, his sentiments.

"Uh-uh, I'm through putting words into your mouth. These have to be your own. I need to hear the words in your heart, Carson."

He wasn't any good at this, she knew that. His eloquence, such as it was, began and ended in the courtrooms he no longer frequented. "You already know them."

Lori shook her head. "Doesn't matter what you think I know or don't know. I have to hear it. To be sure I'm not imagining it."

Carson's dark eyes delved into hers, silently asking for help, for understanding. "You already know what's in my heart."

Maybe she was wrong. Again. Maybe he didn't really care. Maybe what he missed was the familiarity of having her around. If he didn't give her this, then he couldn't give her anything.

"How can I know what's in your heart?" she demanded. "Supposedly until a little while ago, *you* didn't even know what was in your heart. I need to hear the words, Carson."

He took a breath, leaping off the cliff. Risking everything. "I love you."

Tilting her head in his direction, she cupped her ear. Carson's voice had hardly been above a whisper. "Say again?"

A tiny amount of tension eased away. There was a hint of a smile playing on her lips. He glanced up toward the stairs. "I'll wake the baby."

She took a step closer to him. Maybe it was going to be all right after all. "It's worth waking up for."

He slipped his arms around her. "I love you." He waited. She said nothing. "Don't you have anything to say to me?"

Lori lifted her face up to his, a smile in her eyes. "It's about time."

He laughed shortly. She was paying him back. Not that he blamed her. "Don't you have anything else to say to me?"

She couldn't keep the grin back any longer as she fluttered her lashes at him. "You already know what I have to say to you."

He had that coming, Carson thought. "I need to hear the words."

"Yes," she said softly, "you do. We all do." It

was going to be all right. She didn't kid herself, the road ahead was going to be bumpy, but it was going to be all right. "I love you, Carson O'Neill, love you despite the fact that you are very possibly the stubbornest man on the face of the earth." She slipped her arms through his, locking them around his waist. "Love you for your generous heart, your way of never sidestepping a responsibility, and the fact that you are the world's best kisser."

That made him laugh. "How would you know? You haven't kissed the world."

He saw a devilishness enter her eyes just before she asked, "Want me to?"

"Don't even think about it."

He loved her, she thought. He really loved her. She hadn't been wrong and it felt wonderful.

She wanted more. "Why, Carson, why shouldn't I think about it?"

His arms locked tighter around her, bringing her closer to him until their bodies were touching. "Because you're mine."

"And?"

"And I'm yours."

After all this time, it was hard to believe he was finally saying what she'd wanted to hear him say. "Sounds pretty official."

"It will be," he answered matter-of-factly, "once we're married."

He had just succeeded in broadsiding her. She stared at him, wide-eyed. When the man leaped, he really leaped. "When did this happen?"

"It hasn't. Yet." She wanted words, all right, he'd

give her words. "Lori, will you do me the very huge honor of being my wife?"

Excitement, happiness and a host of emotions she couldn't begin to name all welled up inside of her. "I don't know how much of an honor it'll be, but yes, I will. You had me at Lori, you know."

"No, I didn't know. I didn't know anything." God, but he loved her. Why had he been so afraid of letting it out? This was Lori, and he'd always known that she was special. "Maybe that's why it took so long."

She shook her head, negating everything that had come before this moment. "Doesn't matter how long it took. That's behind us. All that matters is now."

"And forever. You still haven't said you'd marry me," he reminded her.

Lori stood up on her toes, her arms just barely reaching around his neck. "I thought that was understood."

He wasn't about to make that mistake again. "From now on, nothing's understood, nothing's taken for granted. Everything's spelled out."

Amusement shone in her eyes. "Could get wordy."

"That's all right," he assured her, "I like the sound of your voice."

"Good thing." Her eyes were smiling at him. "Yes."

"Yes, what?"

"'Yes dear?'" And then she laughed. "Yes, I'll marry you."

He realized that despite everything, he'd been holding his breath until this moment. Until she agreed.

"I'll leave the arrangements up to you. You're good at that sort of thing."

She wasn't about to fall into that trap again. "Uh-uh. From now on, we're doing it all together."

That sounded a great deal better to him than he thought it would have. But then, the fact that the bargain was sealed with a kiss might have had something to do with it.

*   *   *   *   *

If you enjoyed BEAUTY AND THE BABY,
you'll love Marie Ferrarella's next book:
THE BRIDE WORE BLUE JEANS
The last in her series, **The Alaskans**
Available fall 2003
from Silhouette Special Edition

Don't miss it!

Don't miss the latest miniseries from award-winning author Marie Ferrarella:

The MOM SQUAD

Meet...

Sherry Campbell—ambitious newswoman who makes headlines when a handsome billionaire arrives to sweep her off her feet...and shepherd her new son into the world!

A BILLIONAIRE AND A BABY, SE#1528, available March 2003

Joanna Prescott—Nine months after her visit to the sperm bank, her old love rescues her from a burning house—then delivers her baby....

A BACHELOR AND A BABY, SD#1503, available April 2003

Chris "C.J." Jones—FBI agent, expectant mother and always on the case. When the baby comes, will her irresistible partner be by her side?

THE BABY MISSION, IM#1220, available May 2003

Lori O'Neill—A forbidden attraction blows down this pregnant Lamaze teacher's tough-woman facade and makes her consider the love of a lifetime!

BEAUTY AND THE BABY, SR#1668, available June 2003

The Mom Squad—these single mothers-to-be are ready for labor...and true love!

Silhouette®

Where love comes alive™

From *USA TODAY* bestselling author

EMILIE RICHARDS

comes the story of a woman who has played life
by the book, and now the rules have changed.

Faith Bronson, daughter of a prominent Virginia senator and wife
of a charismatic lobbyist, finds her privileged life shattered when
her marriage ends abruptly. Only just beginning to face the lie
she has lived, she finds sanctuary with her two children in a
run-down row house in exclusive Georgetown. This historic
house harbors deep secrets of its own, secrets that force Faith
to confront the deceit that has long defined her.

PROSPECT STREET

"Richards adds to the territory
staked out by such authors as
Barbara Delinsky and Kristin Hannah....
Richards' writing is unpretentious and
effective and her characters burst with
vitality and authenticity."

—*Publishers Weekly*

*Available the first week of June 2003
wherever paperbacks are sold!*

MIRA®

If you enjoyed what you just read,
then we've got an offer you can't resist!

Take 2 bestselling love stories FREE!

Plus get a FREE surprise gift!

Clip this page and mail it to Silhouette Reader Service™

IN U.S.A.
3010 Walden Ave.
P.O. Box 1867
Buffalo, N.Y. 14240-1867

IN CANADA
P.O. Box 609
Fort Erie, Ontario
L2A 5X3

YES! Please send me 2 free Silhouette Romance® novels and my free surprise gift. After receiving them, if I don't wish to receive anymore, I can return the shipping statement marked cancel. If I don't cancel, I will receive 6 brand new novels every month, before they're available in stores! In the U.S.A., bill me at the bargain price of $3.34 plus 25¢ shipping and handling per book and applicable sales tax, if any*. In Canada, bill me at the bargain price of $3.80 plus 25¢ shipping and handling per book and applicable taxes**. That's the complete price and a savings of at least 10% off the cover prices—what a great deal! I understand that accepting the 2 free books and gift places me under no obligation ever to buy any books. I can always return a shipment and cancel at any time. Even if I never buy another book from Silhouette, the 2 free books and gift are mine to keep forever.

215 SDN DNUM
315 SDN DNUN

Name	(PLEASE PRINT)	
Address	Apt.#	
City	State/Prov.	Zip/Postal Code

* Terms and prices subject to change without notice. Sales tax applicable in N.Y.
** Canadian residents will be charged applicable provincial taxes and GST.
All orders subject to approval. Offer limited to one per household and not valid to current Silhouette Romance® subscribers.
® are registered trademarks of Harlequin Books S.A., used under license.

SROM02   ©1998 Harlequin Enterprises Limited

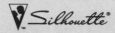

#1672 COUNTERFEIT PRINCESS—Raye Morgan
Catching the Crown

When Crown Prince Marco Roseanova of Nabotavia discovered that Texas beauty Shannon Harper was masquerading as his runaway fiancée, he was furious—until he found himself falling for her. Still, regardless of his feelings, Marco had to marry royalty. But was Shannon really an impostor, or was there royal blood in her veins?

#1673 ONE BRIDE: BABY INCLUDED—Doreen Roberts

Impulsive, high-spirited Amy Richards stepped into George Bentley's organized life like a whirlwind on a quiet morning—chaotic and uninvited. George didn't want romance in his orderly world, yet after a few of this mom-to-be's fiery kisses…order be damned!

#1674 TO CATCH A SHEIK—Teresa Southwick
Desert Brides

Practical-minded Penelope Doyle didn't believe in fairy tales, and her new boss, Sheik Rafiq Hassan, didn't believe in love. But their protests were no guard against the smoldering glances and heart-stopping kisses that tempted Penny to revise her thinking…and claim this prince as her own.

#1675 YOUR MARRYING *HER?*—Angie Ray

Stop the wedding! Brad Rivers had always been Samantha Gillespie's best friend, so she certainly wasn't going to let him marry a woman only interested in his money! But was she ready to acknowledge the desire she was feeling for her handsome "friend" and even—gulp!—propose he marry *her* instead?

#1676 THE RIGHT TWIN FOR HIM—Julianna Morris

Was Patrick O'Rourke crazy? Maddie Jackson had sworn off romance and marriage, so why, after one little kiss, did the confirmed bachelor think she wanted to marry him? Still, beneath his I'm-not-the-marrying-kind-of-guy attitude was a man who seemed perfect as a husband and daddy.…

#1677 PRACTICE MAKES MR. PERFECT—
Patricia Mae White

Police Detective Brett Callahan thought he needed love lessons to lure the woman of his dreams to the altar, so he convinced neighbor Josie Matthews to play teacher. But none of his teachers had been as sweet and seductive as Josie, and *none* of their lessons had evoked passion like this!